It Happened at Lake Louise

Melanie Robertson-King

King Park Press

Published by King Park Press

Copyright © Melanie Robertson-King, 2022
Lake Louise and Chateau: Shutterstock
Couple hugging: Kenny Eliason,
NeONBRAND
(Signed model release on file with NeONBRAND)

It Happened at Lake Louise is a work of fiction. Names,
characters, places and incidents are the product of the
author's imagination or are used fictitiously. Any
resemblance to actual events, locales or persons, living or
dead, is purely coincidental.

ISBN: 978-1-990371-06-6

DEDICATION

For anyone who has suffered through childhood sexual abuse.

ACKNOWLEDGMENTS

Thanks to everyone who put up with my daft questions during the research of this novel. Without your help, the book would not have come to fruition.

I want to thank my niece, Taylor Leigh MacMillan, who provided me with some of the harrowing tales from the Fort McMurray wildfire and suggested a book written by the firefighters who fought the blaze.

Huge thanks to my eagle-eyed proofreader Nancy Chapman.

If I've missed anyone by name, I apologize.

Special thanks to my husband, Don, who continues to support and encourage me, and provides a shoulder to cry on when things don't go well. He redesigned my website making it mobile-friendly and taken charge on the domestic front giving me time to write.

Prologue

Near the Chateau Lake Louise, Alberta

May 18, 2016

"Hello, Abi."

That voice. It couldn't be. He was in prison. That sickening-sweet scent of the cologne he always wore. The one she caught a whiff of earlier, but on someone else. Lori's blood ran cold, as if ice water coursed through her veins. Her heart pounded against her ribcage with enough force to fracture her ribs. Only one person ever used the shortened version of her name. Even her parents called her Abigail. If she was in trouble, then it was Abigail Laurie Brownell.

A growl rumbled from the Great Dane beside her. Her left index finger worked between the stack of bracelets to the raised welts from periods of cutting. It settled in a deep gouge where she took a chunk out of her arm.

Why was he here? Why now? He wasn't the dog's owner, was he? She was to meet that person near the Chateau Lake Louise to ensure the animal's safe return to him and his home in Fort Mac. People came and went in droves here. The phrase safety in numbers suited this place to a T. No way would she have met a stranger at her apartment in Calgary. Who knew what creeps waited to prey on a single white female? She had been a victim as a kid and into her teens. Not anymore. A steady stream of pedestrians strolled by where they stood. They would help her if needed. Wouldn't they?

The individual Lori communicated with via Messenger didn't seem to be the type of person who would cause their pet to react that way. Some people's online personas were opposites of their actual ones. If that were the case here, she wasn't returning the Great Dane. He'd stay with her. She didn't notice the dog turned to face the man behind them. She turned around, her movements awkward from an old injury.

"Unc ... how?" She said, her tongue sticking to the roof of her mouth, making her unable to form the words she wanted to say. Her worst nightmare had come true. She thought she put the past well behind her when she finished school and landed a job as a financial advisor with a major bank in Calgary. Leaving Saskatchewan was not enough.

"Abigail Laurie Brownell. Did you think we'd never find you?"

"My name is Lori Brownlee," she spat. Those words came out too late. Her momentary sense of bravado disappeared. She gave away her true identity with her first reaction. Gawd, sometimes she was so stupid and trusting.

"Aren't you just the cunning little madam?" he sneered. "You still haven't had that ankle fixed. I offered to bring you to the hospital when I found you at the foot of the stairs."

"I fell down the steps because of you. I was trying to get away from you, you pervert."

The canine at her side continued to growl, but the rumblings grew more menacing. Her uncle may have frightened her when she was a child, but not anymore. Yeah right. Lori vibrated with fear as his face loomed before her and the memories of her unhappy, abusive childhood flooded to the surface.

"Lori. Lori Brownlee?" a man's voice called from behind her.

Nervous butterflies flitted about in her stomach as the sour taste of bile worked its way up her throat. Lori's fear of the man standing before her kept her glued to the spot. Unable to take her eyes off him, she didn't spin around. Instead, she said, "Are you Chris? Christopher Scott?"

"Yeah. Sorry, I'm late. Took the wrong exit, then got hung up in the aftermath of an accident that backed the traffic up for miles."

The Great Dane next to her wagged its tail so hard its entire body shook and tugged on her hand, holding the leash.

"Wolfgang! Come here, boy." Chris called.

Lori released the lead, and the dog trotted away. She couldn't bring herself to turn away from her uncle, despite wanting to see Wolfgang's owner. She didn't trust Gary McNeil now and shouldn't have trusted him then. Soon, the Great Dane leaned against her left leg, and a tall man sporting a beard and moustache appeared in her peripheral vision next to his pet.

"Thank you for rescuing Wolfgang. I'd seen clips of him on the television news broadcasts. No one else could get near him but you."

"No problem," she said, her eyes still held fast to the man before them. "I saw him there, too. I tried to team up with the other animal rescue groups, but I was too late. Still, I'm happy I rescued him from the danger zone."

There was something in her expression. Sadness? She had grown attached to the gigantic dog while she cared for him. Was it because she was returning Wolfgang to his owner? No, not that. It was something more profound. Fear? Possible. Of him or the man facing them? Or men? Since his arrival, she hadn't turned and looked at him once.

"You okay?" he asked.

A tiny nod was the response he received. Christopher didn't believe the gesture. Something was amiss. Despite the bright sunshine and the mountainous beauty of the location, a dark cloud of gloom surrounded Lori. A breeze caught her blonde-streaked brown hair and blew it in her face. Her ice-cold hand brushed against his bare arm when she reached to tuck the errant strand behind her ear. A scar, visible now that she secured her hair, followed her hairline for at least two inches. A childhood injury from falling off a bike?

He also carried many battle scars from his youth. Broken bones from playing on the high school football team and stitches from many tumbles from his skateboard and bicycle. The worst, although not visible, resulted from a late Friday afternoon incident when he and his girlfriend, Marianne Lawson, were at the Rideau Centre in downtown Ottawa. She died that day.

After that, Christopher went off the rails. Drinking, partying. Anything to forget about that terrible day. But none of those things worked. They only made him miss Marianne more. One night, between the time of her death and her wake, he and his pals, Ron Smith and Nick Jones, went joyriding in Nick's father's car. They had been drinking before going out. The flashing lights of a cruiser filled the car's interior, and the police arrested the three boys. The shame of his parents picking him up at the station overwhelmed him. He left Ottawa and all its terrible memories not long after that.

The nightmares weren't as frequent anymore. Still, they occurred. The couple's anniversary dates or other noteworthy occasions — their first date. Their first Christmas, the day Marianne died, and her funeral. Sometimes sudden, loud noises propelled him back to that day. A car backfiring. A screen door slamming.

Chris snapped himself out of his reverie. It made no sense to stay in the past, even though he preferred it.

His gaze moved from Lori to the man facing her. Maybe not enough to be siblings, but family, they resembled one another.

"Aren't you going to introduce me to your friend?" the man asked.

"No."

That two-letter word and the emphasis she put behind it spoke volumes.

Christopher suggested they should leave.

"Yes. The sooner I'm out of here, the happier I'll be."

He draped a protective arm around Lori's shoulders, and she spun out from under him. He dropped the limb to his side before they started towards the parking lot where Chris left his truck.

"If you've not experienced it yet, she likes it rough," the man said.

"Who is that creep?"

"M-my uncle."

One

Millennium Lodge, north of Fort McMurray, Alberta

May 3, 2016

Christopher Scott paused near the flat-screen TV mounted to the Millennium Lodge's recreation room wall. News of the wildfire raging to the southwest filled the screen.

No fire burned in the sky. A something inversion, they called it. Temperature? Brown, orange, and red replaced the cerulean closer to the horizon. Vast plumes of smoke rose from the ground as the blaze ravaged everything in its path.

He removed his cell phone from his pocket and took it out of silent mode. Missed calls. Lots of them. Most came from his mother, he discovered when he checked the callers' list. The other, from his neighbour Frank Connolly.

Chris was on his two weeks off when Frank moved into the house across the street. They worked on opposite shift rotations and didn't see each other unless one or the other took vacation. Wolfgang, Chris's Great Dane, needed 'doggie daycare' and more while Chris was onsite at SUNCOR. After he got the puppy, he took him to work. The women employed at the lodge looked after him while he worked. It was an excellent arrangement until Wolfgang outgrew his crate. Frank's two daughters loved the huge lummox.

Pressing the screen on a call from his mother, Chris dialled. "Hi, Ma. What's wrong? You've only called me like a dozen times today."

"I'm worried sick about you, and you not taking my calls hasn't helped."

"Sorry, but you know I can't be on the phone when I'm working. Nothing's wrong with the family?. You're okay?"

"We're all fine, but don't you listen to the news? Watch it on TV?"

"What?" Chris paced back and forth in front of the television.

"Mandatory evacuation. Everyone, especially in your neighbourhood."

He pressed his thumb and fingers against his forehead. "Calm down, Ma. I'm sure it's just a precaution. It'll be fine."

But would it? Is that why Frank called? The men kept communication to a minimum except for pictures of Wolfgang with the children, accompanied by a quick update.

"I missed a call from Frank. Let me return it, and I'll phone you back. Won't take long. Love you. Bye, Ma." Christopher ended his chat with his mother and rang his neighbour. "Hey, Frank, what's this about an evacuation?"

"You heard right. The authorities gave us fifteen minutes to get our stuff together and leave. We planned to take Wolfie with us, but he bolted, and we couldn't find him anywhere. I'm sorry. We had to go."

Christopher swallowed hard and rubbed the back of his collar. The thought of this pet, alone and scared, roaming the streets during a wildfire terrified him. He understood Frank's position. If only his dog weren't so strong-minded. His friend, referring to the animal by his nickname, brought back the memory of when he first met the Connolly family. Becky wasn't quite three years old yet, and she couldn't pronounce Wolfgang or Wolfie. It came out Woofie when she said it.

Although he promised his mother he would call back, Christopher thumbed through the pictures on his mobile, most of which were of Wolfgang. Chris was not a huge fan of social media, but he had a Facebook account. He set it up to keep in touch with his siblings, but used Messenger most of the time.

He chose some recent photos of Wolfie and attached them to the post 'LOST. Answers to the name Wolfgang. Last seen in the Beacon Hill neighbourhood of Fort McMurray.' With luck, someone would find his Great Dane and send a private message to him.

He paced the recreation room, unable to settle his mind for anything other than his missing dog. Chris withdrew to his room. Then he remembered he hadn't called his mother back as promised, so he punched her number into his phone and waited for the call to connect.

"Hi, Ma. I told you I'd get back to you."

"Are you sure you're okay? I mean, with the evacuation and everything."

"I'm at the camp, and we're under no such order here. We're well north of the city." His home was in one of the city's newer suburbs. Beacon Hill had been, or was being, evacuated, no ifs ands or buts. They forced everyone to leave. That's how Wolfgang ended up missing.

"I don't like you working out in the middle of nowhere."

"I'm not in the middle of nowhere, Ma. Besides, I'm a grown man. I've been out here for eons, and you never raised a fuss."

"There has never been a fire threat before like this. The oil sands can be dangerous, too. You know that."

"Plenty of health and safety measures are in place to keep us safe."

"You know I didn't want you to go. Especially so soon after ... Marianne's death."

Chris did not need a reminder. It dogged him all the time. He ran away from the aftermath instead of staying in Ottawa and facing it. Not that he saw anything. The fatal gunshot came from behind them. Worried about his girlfriend's well-being, the whereabouts of the person who fired the shot meant nothing.

His mother stewed and fretted over all her children. The oldest and youngest received the most. None of his brothers and sisters lived in their hometown anymore. Melissa was in New Brunswick. She'd gone to university in Saint John and got a job in the city after graduation. Roger was in Quebec City, and Amy was in Sudbury. At least she stayed in the province, unlike the others. Michael got the farthest from home. He had remained in England after finishing his post-graduate studies and only came home every other year. Those occasions were awesome. All the siblings gathered at their Elm Street home in the nation's capital for a week. Michael stayed on longer because he had more annual leave than the rest. If it worked out, Chris could get four weeks off, but his younger brother was over when he was on his two-week break.

The last time the family was together was at their father's funeral. He succumbed to mesothelioma after years of asbestos exposure. Before that, the unexpected death of Roger's wife.

Christopher was no longer hungry. He wanted a shower and bed. Once settled in his room, he pulled out his wallet and thumbed through to the photo of Marianne. He carried it with him from the day they started dating during his last year of high school at Lisgar Collegiate Institute.

Her auburn hair hung in loose curls to her shoulders, and her green eyes danced with mischief. Chris ached for her, and his eyes filled with tears. Life was so stinking unfair. She was the only victim of the Rideau Centre shooting. They apprehended the shooter a short time later — found him holed up in a washroom.

He sucked in a ragged breath, laid his wallet and her photo on the nightstand, and headed for his shower.

While he stood under the almost scalding spray, Christopher's stomach rumbled. Once he towelled himself dry, he donned a pair of flannel pants and a T-shirt. Chris headed back to check if the cook had left food in the fridge. He was in luck. Only one plate remained. A quarter chicken, mashed potatoes with gravy, and mixed vegetables. On the counter was an assortment of desserts — lemon bars, apple pie, and date squares. He passed on the sweets but warmed his meal in the microwave and sat at a table and caught up with the events on the giant TV.

Nothing much had changed since the earlier reports, except now the cameramen focussed their cameras on the people fleeing the city. One person rode by on a horse, leading another by the reins.

His phone vibrated on the table beside him. Not his mother this time. It wasn't Frank either. He brought the screen to life and found a Facebook message from his youngest sister.

Watching the news. You okay, bro?

Fine for now. The fire isn't near the camp.

What about your house? What about Wolfgang?

A lump formed in Christopher's throat. Despite never meeting him, Melissa was in love with the giant dog. How could he tell her? Wolfie kept him grounded when they were together. The animal missing somewhere amid the destruction taking over Fort Mac gutted him.

Don't care about the house. Can rebuild.

And Wolfgang?

MIA.

He'd said it. He might never see his pet again. Frank did what he had to do: save his family. With any luck, someone fleeing the devastation would rescue the dog.

I'm so sorry. She followed her message with a crying emoji.

Not in the mood for chit-chat, sis. I spoke to Ma, but can you tell the others I'm okay and what's happening?

Sure. Bye, Chris.

Bye Mel.

His appetite, such as it was, vanished. He took his plate to the kitchen, tossed the contents in the bin, and returned to his room. It would be difficult to cope until they found Wolfgang.

Two

Lori's childhood home, Yorkton, Saskatchewan

Late-June, 1988

Weekends and holidays were the worst. Lori was away from her uncle during school sessions.

Lori's father drove transport for Manitoulin and was on the road more than he was home, so her mother found it a blessing when her brother, Gary, came to stay. The woman worked days, Monday to Friday, so was away for at least eight hours each day. Ricky, Lori's older sibling, went to their grandfather's farm and helped during the summer vacation. Other times of the year, he mowed lawns and shovelled snow for the elderly folks in their neighbourhood. That left Lori and her uncle alone in the house.

She found nothing weird in the beginning. The two sat together on the couch and watched television. Sometimes, they were close enough that the man wrapped his arm around her. Once in a while, she perched on his knee, and he held her in his arms. Lori was only a child. How was she to realize it was wrong? When she was on his lap, and he slipped his hand inside the leg of her shorts and his fingers into her panties, she discovered otherwise. She had cuddled with her father, and he

11

never touched her between her legs. Then, the touching stopped for a while. Uncle Gary continued being sweeter than pie to her, but kept his distance. That lasted about a month, and over time, his deviant behaviour escalated. Back then, the word pedophile meant nothing to her. However, she soon put the pieces together when she saw or read about men doing the same things to other little girls as he did to her.

The first time he'd taken her, she was ten. She was getting out of her pyjamas. Before she got her clean underwear on, Gary appeared in her bedroom doorway, stark naked. The sight scared her, but, curious about what this thing was sticking straight out from her uncle's body.

"Touch it," he said.

She shook her head.

"I said touch it." This time, he growled at her.

Afraid of what would happen if she didn't, she reached out and placed her index finger where he demanded.

Before she could react, he laid her on her back and had forced her knees apart. A searing pain shot through her when he pushed inside. She cried and squirmed, trying to escape, but she couldn't.

"There's a good girl, Abi," he crooned afterwards and produced a pink teddy bear. "This is for you. Continue to be a good girl and keep your mouth shut." He turned and left the room.

She bled from the first assault. That frightened her more than what happened.

The thought of telling her parents made Lori sick to her stomach. Her mother thought Gary was all that and a bag of chips. If she told her father, he would thump her uncle and end up in jail. She would be no further ahead than she was now. He had bought her silence this time. From then on, after each encounter, he left a stuffed animal or doll.

"I'm coming in to gather your laundry," Mrs. Brownell announced outside Lori's room before she opened the door.

Lori remained in bed with the covers pulled over her head.

"You not feeling well?"

"No," she said, shaking her head.

Her mother came closer and laid her hand on her forehead. "You're not running a fever." Mrs. Brownell gathered the laundry from the hamper, and as she dumped the clothing into the basket, the blood-spotted underpants fell out.

"Is this why you're upset?" She held the soiled panties out towards her daughter.

"Yes."

"Don't be worried."

"That's easy for you to say."

"You've started menstruating and this will happen once a month. Your body is telling you you're old enough to have a baby. Each month it prepares ... oh, never mind. I'll be right back."

Baby? Could she? That terrified her more than anything else. Her mother returned with a box of pads and a book. "This explains things better than I can. You read it, and we'll talk about it when I come back. Are you still bleeding? The first time, a few spots is usually all there is."

"Dunno."

"Take a clean pair of panties to the bathroom. I'll put your dirty ones in the wash and come back to help you."

The washroom was downstairs, right inside the back door. Lori crept down the stairs and sat on the toilet. Bloodstains dotted this underwear, too. She took them and her pyjama bottoms off and slipped the clean undies on, but left them puddled at her ankles. She had to get back to her room.

"You gonna be all day in there?" Ricky banged on the door.

"Go away."

"You're not the only one who lives in this house. I need to go."

"Richard, leave your sister be. Can I come in, Abigail?"

"Yes."

Mrs. Brownell entered the bathroom. She helped Lori affix the pad to her underwear and wrapped a towel around her. "I'll put these in the wash. You get dressed, and then we'll eat breakfast. I remember my first time. I was scared, too."

Lori stuck her tongue out at her older brother as she left the room.

Her cousin Janey McNeil had invited her to spend two weeks with her and her mother at their home in Regina to celebrate their thirteenth birthdays. The girls were born a week apart. Would her parents allow her to go? They weren't ogres, but they were strict. They had no clue what was happening since Gary came to live with them.

Her aunt and uncle had separated before he moved into the Brownell home. Did the reason have something to do with what he was doing to her? Maybe he never said why?

The night Janey extended the invitation, Lori's father was home for a few days. The timing couldn't have been better, so she asked for permission. She was extra helpful that night, doing things for her mother that were not expected of her.

When they sat down for their meal, she began. "Janey invited me to Regina. Aunt Cindy says she's fine with me staying with them."

Gary dropped his knife with a clatter.

"Oh, Abigail. I don't know," her father said. "Regina is not small like Yorkton."

"Da-ad. I'm almost thirteen. Why not?"

"You have been nowhere alone other than here."

"I won't be on my own. Aunt Cindy and Janey will be with me.

"How would you get there?" Lori's mother asked.

"There are trains and buses. I'll find a way. Believe me, I need to go."

"Abigail Laurie Brownell, that's it. I gave you my answer."

Lori threw her napkin on the table and fled to her room. Her father didn't understand how important this vacation was to her. She flew up the stairs, slammed the door and flung herself on the bed. She would go crazy if she didn't leave. Her uncle pestered her all the time, but for the most part, she kept him at bay.

A soft knock sounded. "It's me."

Her mother's voice. At the supper table, she didn't defend nor approve the invitation.

"Come in." Lori swiped the tears away with the backs of her hands. She turned and faced the door.

"This trip means a great deal to you, doesn't it?" Mrs. Brownell sat beside her and massaged Lori's back.

"You don't know how much."

"I'll try talking to your father later. See if I can't persuade him to change his mind."

"Th-thank you."

After her mother exited, she pulled up her sweater sleeve and rubbed her fingers over her wrist. Lori started cutting herself a few years ago, and the scars left white ridges on her skin. If she didn't leave Yorkton, she didn't know what she would do. She didn't have many friends at school, nor was she close to her brother Ricky. To him, she was the little sister who wanted to tag along.

Later that evening, after the house was quiet, Mrs. Brownell poured her husband a coffee and sat at the kitchen table with him. "Put the paper down, Bert."

"What is it, Sue?"

"I think you were too harsh with Abigail. She's not a child anymore. We can't protect her forever. I think we should let her spend time with Janey. The girls haven't seen one another in ages. It will do them both the world of good."

"Are you undermining my decision?"

"No. Of course not. You wouldn't object if Ricky was going."

"He's a lad and two years older than Abigail." He added two more heaping spoonfuls of sugar to his coffee. "What?"

"Bert, you'll end up a diabetic if you keep using that much sugar." Lori's mother picked up the container, placed it on the counter out of her husband's reach, then poured his dark roast down the sink. She replaced it with a fresh cup she'd sweetened — far less than he consumed.

He sipped and spluttered. "This is disgusting. I need the extra sugar to drink that strong coffee you make, Susan."

"Fine then. From now on, make your own. I don't care. I care about our daughter and us allowing her to see her cousin. You can poo-poo it all you want, but I'm sending her. Something's been bothering her, and she won't talk to me about it. I ask, and she clams up. It will do her good. I can pay her return bus fare from my tips stash."

Susan stood and reached into the upper cabinet for the brown jar she put her change in when she came home. It didn't rattle as it should, and it didn't weigh as much as it did the last day she had deposited the handful of coins in it. With trepidation, she unscrewed the lid. Empty. Every cent of her money had vanished. She collapsed on her chair.

"Abigail! Richard!" Mr. Brownell bellowed. "Both of you, in the kitchen."

Within seconds, the children stood in the room.

"What's up, Dad?" Ricky asked.

"Tips. Your mother's tips. Did either of you take her cash?"

"N-no," they said in unison.

"You best not be lying. Someone cleaned out your mother's hard-earned tips, and when I find out who, there will be hell to pay."

"It wasn't me." Lori fled the room in tears.

"Me neither." Ricky was hot on her heels.

"I believe them, Bert. They didn't take the money."

"How about that shiftless brother of yours? He was supposed to stay a few weeks. A month at the most. And how long has it been? Over three years. Three years, Susan. I'm getting fed up with him being here."

"I'll speak with him."

"You better. I suppose now I'll have to come up with the bus fare and spending money for Abigail's trip."

"Some days, Bert, you can be a real curmudgeon."

"What was that all about, sis?" Ricky asked when they were out of their parents' earshot.

"Beats me. I've never once gone near Mom's tips." Lori sank to the floor at the head of the stairs.

Her brother joined her. "That makes two of us, then. I didn't realize she even got them working at Tim Hortons."

"That's because you're never home when she gets home from work."

"I have an after-school job."

"So, if you didn't touch them, and I didn't go near them. Dad wouldn't. That only leaves Uncle Gary." A shudder travelled down her spine. He was disgusting, but was he a thief? The stuffed animals. The dolls. "You don't …" Lori stopped before she said something she would regret.

"You think mom's brother is ripping her off?"

"He's here all day, every day. What does he do when we're not home?" She knew what he did when she was alone with him.

"Can't be. Mom gave him a place to stay when Aunt Cindy kicked him out."

"I wish she hadn't," Lori mumbled.

"You don't like him?"

"No. Besides, you wouldn't get it." Lori stood, walked into her room, and closed the door behind her.

Lori flopped on her bed. She *had* to go see Janey. If not, she would burst or worse. Then, a soft knock sounded on her door.

"Abigail, it's Mom. Can I come in?"

"Yes."

Mrs. Brownell tiptoed into the room. "I talked your father around. You can go to Regina and spend the time with Janey and your aunt."

"Thank you." Lori flung her arms around her mother's neck and hugged her. While she was in the woman's soft embrace, she asked, "Do you know why Uncle Gary and Aunt Cindy split up?"

"He never said."

"I do."

Her mother loosened her grip on her shoulders and held Lori back at arm's length. "You do?"

"Yes. Uncle Gary's … he's an evil man. He's been molesting me, and I don't like it."

"Don't be ridiculous. Gary wouldn't do that. He's my brother."

"He would, and he has. I don't care if you believe me; I know the truth. We talked about inappropriate touching in health class."

Lori's last sentence earned her a slap across the face. "Don't you ever speak that way about your uncle again."

Palm on her stinging cheek, she nodded.

"You're just lucky I'm still letting you go to Regina. If the wrong person heard you, do you know what sort of trouble you would cause Gary?"

Stunned, Lori curled up on her bed with her back to her mother. The reaction was what she expected.

Three

July 2015

The doctors diagnosed his father with cancer three months before his death. At least his father had a will, and registered the house, bank accounts, and car in both their names. Christopher came home in late April for two weeks. His father didn't look sick then.

He didn't recognize him when he returned in July before the funeral. He had wasted away to mere skin and bones. While the man loved all five of his children, Mel was *the apple of his eye,* most likely because Melissa came along well after the others. Chris was thirteen when his mother gave birth to her. Then, after his younger twin siblings were born, his mother suffered a miscarriage. So welcoming a bouncing baby girl into the Scott clan was unexpected.

Chris was the eldest and named after his paternal grandfather; Roger, the second born, after his maternal grandfather. Tradition ended there. To the best of his knowledge, Michael or the girls weren't named after a family member.

Melissa perched on the edge of a sofa in the corner, shredding a tissue; her eyes red-rimmed and bloodshot from crying.

Chris walked over and gave his sister a brotherly hug. "Your makeup will run if you keep it up." He took a fresh one from the box while taking the remnants of the one she held away from her.

"Funny, ha ha." Mel took the new Kleenex and blew her nose.

The twins, Michael and Amy, sat together near the fireplace. A big-screen television, mounted on the wall above the gas-fired flame, showed a video of various family photographs from their father's life. Roger stood with their mother, speaking to someone Christopher didn't recognize.

"Dad, I'm hungry," Adam, Chris's seven-year-old nephew, whined to his father.

"Don't interrupt when we're talking," Roger said, scolding his son.

His mom and brother spoke with the head caterer. A short time later, the catering staff, dressed in black trousers and crisp white shirts, set up a spread of assorted-filling sandwiches, cheese, crackers, squares and cookies on the large table in the centre of the room. Another person from this group placed a coffee urn on a side table with cream, sugar, styrofoam cups and wooden stir sticks.

Christopher helped Melissa to her feet and led her to the food. He held her plate while she put a couple of small egg salad sandwiches on it. His stomach growled. How long since he last ate? The entire family had just gone through the motions. No one took an interest in anything during the few days between the death and the funeral.

As an adult, Chris had attended three funerals. The first was Marianne's, and her mother acted as if she didn't want him there. It was as if she blamed him for her dying. The second was Roger's wife's suicide. And now his father's cancer. He hoped the next one wouldn't be soon since these last two were only a year apart.

That evening, back at the Scott family home on Elm Street, Chris's siblings prepared for their departures the following morning. His mother sat in the armchair beside the one her husband always occupied. A small side table stood between them. She nursed a cup of tea.

"Let me get you another one. That one must be cold by now." Christopher took the mug to the kitchen. He came back with a fresh, steaming one. "Here you go."

"The house will be so empty after you all leave tomorrow." Mrs. Scott dabbed at her eyes with a tissue. "I'll be rattling around in the house by myself."

"I'm not leaving yet, Ma. There are still things that need settling. I'll stay until I'm done."

"I'm glad your father named you executor of his estate. You're the responsible one. You've always been the level-headed one."

"I wouldn't go that far." He started to sit in his father's chair, but paused about halfway down.

"Go ahead, Christopher. Your father isn't going to need it anymore." She burst into tears.

Guilt washed over him. "I didn't mean to make you cry." He strode to her side and rubbed her shoulders. His parents' forty-fifth wedding anniversary was last month. Four and a half years after their marriage, his mother had Christopher. "I know things are different from back in the seventies, but why did you and dad wait to start a family?"

Again, she lifted the tissue to her eyes. "We didn't."

Christopher shook his head. "You got married in 1970, and I wasn't born until late 1974. That's a long time to me."

"You were our first who lived."

Chris's jaw dropped. This was the first he'd heard of children — at least one child older than him. "We don't need to discuss this now. Between me trying to sit in dad's chair , and asking dumb questions, I didn't intend to upset you, so let's leave it for the time being."

His mother nodded and sipped her tea.

Later that evening, Mrs. Scott asked, "Christopher, would you ask the others to come down here, please?"

"Sure, Ma," he said as he strode to the foot of the stairs.

"Don't yell from there. Go upstairs."

Why do men think they have to yell to get attention? Her late husband did that. He stood at the base of the steps and shouted for the kids. It didn't matter the occasion. Or if it was to find out who did what to whom.

Within moments, her children gathered in the living room.

"What's up, Mom?" asked Melissa.

"Yeah, what?" Amy piped up.

Roger and Michael looked confused, but remained silent.

"Your brother ... Christopher asked me a question earlier, and I'd just as soon only have to answer it once."

The matriarch of the Scott family walked to the console table and pulled a fancy wooden box from the drawer. She placed it on her lap when she sat in her chair.

"Christopher asked why your father and I waited so long to have children. We were married in 1970, and he didn't come along until December 1974. I told him we hadn't, but that he was the first who lived."

"Mom, what are you saying?" Melissa interrupted. "You mean we had another brother or sister?"

"Your father forbade me to talk about it. I think the tragedy hurt him far more than me — not that I didn't suffer, too. We had a daughter born in 1972. She was flawless — ten fingers, ten toes. Full term, but stillborn."

"Oh, Mom." Amy hugged her mother.

She patted her daughter's hand and beckoned her to sit.

Amy pulled the footstool over, and she and Melissa shared it. Her three sons stood behind them. Roger with his hands in his pockets; Michael with his on his twin's shoulders; Chris with his arms folded across his chest.

"Her name was Evelyn, after my mother. We called her Evie. Everything was fine. Sometime between my last weekly check-up and her birth, she died." Mrs. Scott opened the case. Inside was a white leather Bible. "The funeral home gave us this." She plucked a tissue from the container beside her and dabbed her eyes before lifting the book from its resting place. A small photograph lay on the bottom, along with documents pertaining to her child's non-life.

She handed the photo to Chris. "The undertakers took this for me. I couldn't let her go without having some record of it. The official cause of her death was …" Mrs. Scott paused, overwhelmed by the situation. That fateful day in November 1972. She was back on that date now. "She asphyxiated because something wound the umbilical cord around her neck."

Christopher inspected the photograph. His mother was right. This tiny human, his older sister, appeared perfect. His mother was speaking again, but the image he held engrossed him. He stared at it for a few seconds longer, then passed it on to Michael.

"We don't need to know more if it's too hard for you. You've told us everything that's important," he said as he squatted facing the woman.

"Your father acted as if he shut it out of his mind. Many a year on November 3rd, I caught him with this box on the table, holding the picture of his daughter in his hand; his shoulders shaking. I knew he was crying, but never let on."

"Where is Evie? I mean, where's her grave?" Roger asked.

"Pinecrest."

"I think we should go before we go home and pay our respects to the sister we never knew existed," said Amy.

"Michael, do you have time before you catch your flight back to Manchester?" asked Melissa.

"If we go early tomorrow, then yes."

"You'll come with us, Ma?"

"Yes, I'll come, too."

Four

Lori's apartment, Calgary Alberta

May 3, 2016

Lori switched on the television when she got home from work. It had been one of those days. Every customer complained about something. Their investments took a hit. It was too hot, and they needed rain — all well beyond her capacity as a financial advisor. She didn't have a crystal ball, nor was she clairvoyant and could see or predict the stock markets or the weather.

The fire raging in Fort McMurray filled the news. A ticker at the bottom of the screen announced the evacuation. Cars, trucks and motorcycles clogged the streets as people tried to flee the inferno. The red sky wasn't from a sailor's delight sunset from the saying. In this case, the flames devouring everything in their path caused the crimson glow, shrouded by smoke and ash. Her stomach growled while she stood transfixed in the middle of the room, reminding her she didn't eat lunch.

On a normal day, her schedule held fewer appointments,

and she ate. However, one of her colleagues called in sick, so she took on some of those clients besides her own. Lori picked up her insulated bag from the coffee table and headed to the kitchen.

The Greek salad she packed that morning still appeared fit for human consumption, so she put her other things away. Afterwards, Lori poured the vinaigrette dressing over it, returned to the living room, and plopped on the low-slung IKEA sofa. Between mouthfuls, she clicked through the channels to search for something else. Her viewing choices were tacky commercials or news — nothing resembling escapism. When one of the local stations came back from a break, it had nothing to do with the blaze, but something different. She turned up the volume and right away wished she hadn't. Pedophile, that one word, brought it all back.

Lori dropped her salad container on the table, dashed to the apartment's entrance, put the chain on the latch, and leaned back against the door. Her heart pounded, and beads of sweat formed on her forehead. It was happening again. Whenever stories of this nature made the news, they propelled her back to her childhood and Uncle Gary.

In this case on the television, the guards found the creep dead in his prison cell of an alleged suicide. No justice there. But, if the other prisoners made his death appear that way, then bully for them.

She cast her eyes on her wrists, covered by long sleeves, lots of bracelets on her right, and a chunky watch on her left. Beneath the coverings lay scars, raised white welts from years of cutting herself. Anything handy worked. Scissors, razor blades, plastic knives, kitchen knives, fingernails.

Later that evening, Lori drew herself a bubble bath. She climbed into the hot, foamy water and lay in its embrace before sinking below the surface. If Lori were dead, the pain, and suffering she endured, thanks to her uncle, would go away. She yanked herself up out of the water breathless, and sputtering, unable, to stay under long enough to finish the job.

Lori took her razor from the shelf on the tub surround and shaved her legs. Rattled by the news from earlier, she sliced herself. "Blast!" Drops of her blood formed swirling tendrils as they sank into the water. She gave herself an almighty gash.

What could she accomplish if she did it on purpose, if she cut herself that badly by accident? For the longest time, Lori held the shaver over her wrist. Did she? Didn't she? In the end, she finished shaving her legs and got out of the tub.

Her scars disgusted her, not to mention reminded her of the abuse meted out by her uncle within months of him moving in with her family. Before Gary arrived on the scene, she was a cheerful child. She became a loner, sullen and suspicious of everyone. The male population of the schools she attended withstood her suspicions. Her father and Ricky were the only men she trusted.

Lori's parents and brother no longer knew her whereabouts, thanks to the help from her cousin Janey. During her last year at Yorkton Regional High School, she looked at colleges and universities out of the province. After a great deal of research, she decided on Lakeland College in Lloydminster, Alberta.

The trouble was she had to apply to these institutions using her birth name. Otherwise, there was no proof of the excellent grades she'd achieved. Lori may have been a loner, but she was smart. She immersed herself in her studies and scored top marks in all her subjects. She changed her name from Abigail Laurie Brownell to Lori Brownlee within her first months at Lakeland and disappeared.

Uncle Gary went to jail after her and Janey's fourteenth birthdays. Not soon enough for her liking, but at least they put him away. She'd deal with his release if the time came. So far, there had been no parole hearings she was aware of, but they would have notified the girl she was before, not the one she became.

Lori wondered if the police ever called Janey to give a victim impact statement as the conclusion of her uncle's prison sentence approached. Janey never mentioned it, if they had. The last time she spent time with her was when she travelled to

Regina to change her name over twenty years ago. Janey's physical health was terrible, and her mental health was worse. Abuse, denial, blackmail and bribery messed with their heads. They found different ways to come to terms with what that man subjected them to as young girls.

Five

Lori's childhood home, Yorkton, Saskatchewan

Mid-July 1988

Lori placed her packed bag near the door before six o'clock that morning. She couldn't escape from the house fast enough and hoped she would be on the bus by the time her uncle woke up.

Since Ricky left for Grandpa Brownell's farm, unless her father was on his days off, she was on her own in the house with Uncle Gary. He would leave her alone if she told him it was that time of the month. But she worried if on the times he didn't, about getting pregnant.

"All ready?" Her mother asked. "I'll drop you at the station on my way to work."

Lori nodded.

Mr. Brownell had said his goodbyes to her the night before. He had a load with an early pick up today and left the house before sunrise.

The mother and daughter were about to leave the house when Gary appeared. "What's this? Do I not get to say goodbye to my favourite niece?"

"Only niece," Lori said.

"Give me a hug, then."

It was the last thing she wanted to do, but her mother pushed her towards him.

He enveloped her in a bear hug and placed his mouth close to her ear. "Don't tell anyone about our times together," he said, hissing, "or I might hurt your mother or father."

The thought of her uncle doing something that evil terrified her. She squeezed her eyes closed as an image of her parents being injured entered her mind.

On her way to the bus station, Lori sat with her arms folded across her chest and scowled.

"What's wrong with you? In the beginning, you were excited about going away for a few weeks, and now ... well, now you're in a mood."

She had to say something since she couldn't tell her mother. "I told you last night. I don't like Uncle Gary living with us. He touches me in places he shouldn't."

"What's brought that on? You always act like you like him and like having him here. He spoils you rotten. I've seen the things he's bought you."

"Did Aunt Cindy ever say why she kicked him out?"

"No. I never spoke to her — only to Gary when he showed up on our doorstep. He's my brother. I couldn't turn him away. Why do you ask?" Mrs. Brownell flipped on the signal light and turned into the station's parking lot.

"No reason. Just curious."

The bus pulled in not long after they arrived.

Just before Lori boarded the coach, her mother hugged her goodbye. "Have fun with Janey, behave for your aunt."

"Ask Uncle Gary about your tip money. I think he used the cash to pay for everything he bought me." Lori found a seat by the window. She waved to her mother until the woman was out of sight.

Why did Abigail suggest she ask Gary about her missing tips? Her brother wouldn't take it. What about the accusations of the man touching her daughter in inappropriate places? The questions dogged Sue Brownell all day at work. When her shift ended, she sighed with relief. She had suffered a terrible day. She saw her daughter off to Regina and then Abigail accused her sibling of being a thief.

The house looked lonely when she pulled into the driveway. Ricky left for his grandfather's farm once school finished for the summer. Bert was working. It was only her and Gary.

The television was on when Sue walked by the front window. Her brother would be in his usual position on the sofa. She checked the mailbox on her way by, then opened the door.

Gary was on the couch snoring, as she suspected. When he first came to stay, he helped by doing housework and grocery shopping on non-regular days. The last couple of years, he had slacked off pitching in and earning his keep. She slammed the door shut, sending him into a mass of flailing arms and legs.

"What did you do that for?"

Sue smiled at him. "No reason other than to watch you jump."

"Not funny. Get Abi off on the bus, okay?"

"Yes. This trip will be good for Abigail. Something's been bothering her for ages. I don't suppose you know?" Sue said as she hung her purse on the hall tree. She knew what her daughter said. What would her brother say?

"N-no," Gary said. There would be dire consequences if she said anything. If the little madam crossed him, Abi would pay for that indiscretion when she came home.

"Have you been dipping into my tip jar?" Sue asked.

He followed her to the kitchen. "Why? Did Abi say I did?"

"Not in so many words. She thought you might know what happened. Who cleaned out all the change?"

His niece should be face to face with him, not his sister. He'd fix her, ratting him out to her mother. He flexed his fingers and coiled them into fists. A cold sweat formed on his upper lip, and he swiped it away with the back of his hand. "Why don't I make you a brew, sis? I think you're missing Abi."

Gary picked up the kettle, filled it and plugged it in. While waiting for it to boil, he gathered the instant coffee, milk and sugar and grabbed two clean mugs off the drainboard. Susan worked at Tim Hortons. Could she not bring some home from there so they could drink *real* coffee instead of the freeze-dried crap she kept in the house?

No way could he tell his sister he took the money. That he bought presents for Abi with it. He couldn't tell Sue what the occasions were. It was bad enough the woman had likely seen the stuffed animals and dolls in Abi's room or closet. Dear Abi would be sorry when she came home.

Six

The Scott family home, Ottawa, Ontario

July 2015

Melissa walked to the window. A dead pigeon lay on the pavement as a car stopped on the opposite side. The driver emerged and picked up the deceased bird. "Chris, come here. You must see this."

Her older brother, and the rest of the family, strode to Melissa's side. "That car just drove the other way. The guy hit that pigeon."

"Why return to the crime scene?"

"Amy, you read too many police procedurals," Chris teased.

The man started towards the Scott residence, clutching the bird at arm's length.

"Where's he going?" Roger asked.

Chris strode into the foyer with Melissa hot on his heels and flung the door open. "Where are you headed with that?"

"Your garbage can."

"No, you're not," Chris said, still dressed in his shirt and tie, as he stepped outside to the porch. "Been enough death here of late. We just buried my father earlier today."

The man holding the pigeon squirmed. "S-sorry," he said.

"I don't care what you do with the dead bird, but you're not leaving it here."

Melissa joined her brother. "Weird." It had been that kind of day. First and most important of all, their father's funeral. Chris fibbed when he said they buried their father, but it got the point across to the man. She and the others never knew that her older sister existed. Now this.

While they stood together, Chris put his arm around Melissa's shoulders. He was the family's rock despite that solidity being crushed after his girlfriend, Marianne's, murder. Mel liked her, and she took her death hard.

Satisfied, he took the feathered corpse away; Melissa turned towards the house and walked back inside. Chris stayed outside longer.

"Can you believe the nerve of that guy? Going to throw the dead pigeon in our garbage can. Chris told him where to get off."

"I'll go back out later, make sure he didn't sneak back and drop it in there, anyway."

"Ooh ... a body dump location. Are you going to examine the bin for evidence?" Amy asked.

Melissa giggled, and soon the entire family guffawed and snorted.

After breakfast, everyone piled into two vehicles. Neither one was large enough for all six of them. Chris took Mrs. Scott and Melissa with him, and Roger took Amy and Michael. "We'll meet you at the cemetery — just inside the gates on Baseline. We all know where Pinecrest is, but Ma is the only one who knows where Evie's grave is."

"Let's take some of dad's flowers," Melissa suggested. She jumped back out of Chris's truck and dashed into the house. She returned with a bouquet of white roses. While it occupied her, the others left.

"Are you sure you wouldn't have been better riding with Roger, Ma? His car is lower than this."

"I'm fine. I'm not old and decrepit yet."

"It's okay to take these, Mom? If you would rather, I'll get some from another bouquet."

"They're lovely. Evie will love them."

"Sorry, there isn't much space. You gonna be all right, Mel?"

"You betcha."

Chris started the engine, shifted into drive, and soon they were merging onto the Queensway, or as Mr. Scott used to call it, the Squeezeway.

When they arrived at the cemetery, Roger and his passengers waited at the edge of the road inside the entrance. Chris steered around Roger's car and took the lead, with his mother giving him directions to the mausoleum where his sister's ashes rested.

"Your father's ashes should be interred here, too. However, he wanted no part of it. He never said why, but I think it was because of the way he reacted to Evie's death. So where is he? At home on the mantle. Something else for me to dust."

"I guess he didn't want you to be bored, Ma, being in the house by yourself." Chris stifled a chuckle. Some days, his sense of humour was macabre.

Pinecrest was an enormous graveyard. You could get lost if you didn't know your way around. He hoped his mother remembered the way. No signage to show he was going the wrong direction, so that was a positive. There weren't many vehicles there.

"Pull off anywhere here, son," Mrs. Scott said.

A wall with polished, rectangular, red granite blocks, some with flower urns attached, stood on the left. Chris exited the truck, then helped his mother down from the passenger seat. Roger pulled up behind them and the others piled out of his car. The vaults were different sizes which was not how they first appeared.

Mrs. Scott walked straight to the wall, took two steps to

her right, and placed her hand on a block. "Right here, kids."

The engraving on the granite read:

Evelyn "Evie" Scott
b. Nov 3, 1972
d. Nov 3, 1972

Flowers, although wilted, were in the urn on the face of his sister's vault. Someone visited within the last few days.

"I come once a week since her birth. Your father never knew. Even when he got sick and required more care, I still came. I needed a respite worker so I could leave the house. Your father — everything. I caught the bus and came down. Picked up a bouquet after I left the house."

"Ah, Ma. You shouldn't have had to sneak around like that," Chris said and wrapped his arm around his mother's shoulders.

Melissa removed the old blooms and replaced them with the white roses pilfered from one of the few bunches of flowers they took home from the funeral home.

One by one, Chris's siblings stepped forward and placed their palm on the face of their late sister's vault. He waited until the end. This was all too reminiscent of Marianne's funeral.

After the cemetery visit, everyone resumed their departure routines. Roger was driving Melissa as far as Quebec City. From there, she was going by train and bus to Saint John. "Do you want me to take you to the bus station, Amy?"

"Sure. I'd love it."

"What about you, Mike? Can I drop you at the airport?"

"No, you're good bro. Got a limo ordered."

"Aren't you just hoity-toity," Melissa teased.

"On my expense account, Baby Girl."

Chris enjoyed his time at home with his brothers and sisters. Whether he wanted to admit it or not, he missed them all and their familiar banter. It was a lonely life he chose for himself. Since Marianne's death, he had become withdrawn. He socialized little with his neighbours, just the odd beer in the front yard on a hot day.

After Roger loaded his car, he and the girls hugged everyone else goodbye. Michael's limo arrived, and he said his goodbyes.

It was just him and his mother now. Being executor meant staying behind and completing as many tasks as possible before heading home. He'd return to Fort Mac after that.

Chris sat at the dining room table with a shoebox of documents before him. Somehow, he would make sense of the jumble so he could file his father's last tax return. Cheque stubs — both incoming and outgoing — receipts for everything from medical supplies to grocery store cash register slips, bank statements and bills. He hoped they paid the latter.

The easiest way to handle the mess was to separate everything into piles. He wrote labels for the stacks on a sheet of plain white paper and laid them out. Incoming cheque stubs/payment vouchers, outgoing cheque stubs, medical and prescription receipts, bank statements, bills. Some medications his father took were one hundred percent covered, while some only partially and others not at all. He didn't know about the oxygen machine. He would worry about that once he organized the paperwork.

"Ma, how did Dad ever figure out his taxes?"

"He didn't. He kept everything in a box and come tax time he took it to the accountant."

Chris shook his head. The person tasked with filing the return deserved a medal.

"Do you have copies of the previous years' returns?" He kneaded the back of his neck. Sorting this mess out would be a gargantuan process.

"Here you go," Mrs. Scott said as she sat down a plastic tote.

The contents in individual folders were visible through the semi-transparent lid. "Thanks, Ma."

Once he had the papers from the shoe box stacked in their proper piles, he lifted the lid from the container and removed a folder. He took it to the living room and sat in his father's armchair, where he opened it. He was hoping a completed tax return with the receipts would help with the one he had to complete now. Chris excelled in math during school and used it every day on the job. This financial math was doing his head in and he had just got started.

Chris leaned back in the chair. This was not the best day to tackle this project, but he had begun. Thankfully, the house had an eat-in kitchen, so he could leave the paperwork on the dining room table until he was done.

"Ma, I'm going out for a bit. You be okay until I get back?"

"Yes, I'll be fine. Off you go."

Chris climbed into his truck. He could have flown home in a fraction of the time, but was glad he travelled in his own vehicle back to Ottawa. The Cadillac sat in the narrow driveway. His father was so proud when he brought it home. Prior to that, they owned a station wagon and everyone piled into it on family vacations and picnics. In the rear, in the backseat and sometimes at least one kid up front in the middle between their parents. Had Evie lived, she would have been with them.

It must have been hard on his mother being forbidden to talk about it. She had to sneak off to the cemetery to leave flowers. Finding out at forty you had an older sister was a shock. And then to discover she was stillborn. It made him happy that his mother had a photo to remember her and the vault in the mausoleum she could visit.

He started the engine and put the truck in gear. For the longest time, Christopher cruised around his old neighbourhood. Past Lisgar Collegiate. Past the childhood homes of his buddies Nick Jones and Ron Smith. Marianne's funeral was the last time he saw them. Past Marianne's house. Why he came down Arthur Street was beyond him. He had avoided her house or the nearby area since the shooting.

After driving for ages, he found himself on Prince of

Wales Drive, headed out of the city, farther than Merivale and Woodroffe, but not as far as the Chevy dealership. Chris pulled into the memorial gardens' driveway and stopped. Why did he come here? Hadn't he seen enough death and funeral homes these past few days?

Could he even remember where Marianne's grave was located? January 5, 2000 was a cold sunny day. A piercing wind blew while they stood in silence and the minister performed the graveside service. Fifteen years later and Chris still felt Mrs. Lawson's eyes bore through him. He squirmed in his seat at the memory, rubbed his neck, and drove towards the back of the graveyard. A lot had changed since then.

Shame washed over him as he continued through the green space. On his trips home over the years, he could have visited her grave, but he didn't. It was a bitter reminder of that New Year's Eve when that freak gunned Marianne down.

Brass plaques laying flat on the ground marked the graves and memorialized the deceased, unlike at Pinecrest where most of the stones stood upright. Her parents decided where they buried their daughter, not him. He would have preferred elsewhere.

As he rounded the next bend, a funeral cortege parked along the road. He didn't want to see the mourners gathered nearby. But death never took a holiday as far as he knew, so why should today be any different? He crept past the line of cars so not to disturb the sombre event.

Chris located an area that seemed familiar to him. He pulled the truck over and shut off the engine. After a delay, he walked across the grass and read the names until he came to the plaque marked 'Lawson'. The vase held flowers that were past their prime. Mr. or Mrs. Lawson must have left them.

Chris admonished himself for not stopping to pick up any. Even a grocery store bouquet was better than nothing. He kneaded his neck and drew in a ragged sigh. Tears pricked his eyes. If it wasn't for him, she wouldn't be here. He'd never been able to move past that.

Seven

Yorkton to Regina, Saskatchewan

Mid-July 1988

The scenery passed by the window as the bus sped along the roads. Lori saw a mileage distance sign at one point, but they passed by too fast for her to read it. When the driver announced the next stop was Regina, she started gathering her belongings, and sighed. She spent most of her home time looking over her shoulder trying to avoid her uncle who seemed to lurk everywhere and scrutinize her every move.

Aunt Cindy and Janey were waiting outside the terminal, when the coach pulled in. Her cousin had changed. They both had. Whatever weight Janey lost, Janey's mother gained. She got it that her aunt would gain weight after breaking up with her husband. Her own mother put on a few pounds, too, over the years. Maybe it was just an age thing.

"Did you have a pleasant trip?" Aunt Cindy asked.

"Yes. I was afraid when you first invited me, my parents would say no. Dad did, but Mom talked him into letting me come." She hugged them both and pulled her sleeves back to their proper position.

"The car is just over here. I'll take your suitcase, Abigail. You two girls can sit in the back together. You must have lots to catch up on."

They walked across the parking lot to an older compact Chevy. Luggage stowed, and everyone buckled in; they worked their way into the traffic and back to Aunt Cindy's and Janey's apartment.

Lori was positive they lived in a house when she last came to Regina, but said nothing.

"I'll put your bag in my room," Janey said. "Come on, and I'll show you around."

The tour of the tiny place didn't take long.

"I thought I would cook pizza for supper your first night here. It's only a frozen one. I hope that's okay."

Lori's stomach clenched. Gary fed her that as a treat after one time. She squeezed her eyes shut, trying to erase the memory. "As long as there aren't any peppers." The one Gary cooked contained green peppers, which she detested, but he forced her to eat them, anyway. She ended up violently ill.

"I think we're safe, honey. One is pepperoni. The other Hawaiian. Why don't you two listen to music or talk about boys, whatever thirteen-year-old girls do these days? I'll pop the pizzas in when the oven's hot and call you when they're ready."

Janey's room was pink and white. Pink roses on the curtains, pink flowers on the bedspread and pillow shams, and pink walls — even the lampshades were Pepto Bismol pink! It was a sharp contrast to Lori's plain grey room. Lori didn't care for this flowery stuff. This was a time capsule of Janey's childhood.

"Do you like Backstreet Boys?" Janey asked as she riffled through her collection of cassette tapes.

"They're all right," Lori said, not wanting to hurt her cousin's feelings, and sat on the bed and scanned the room. At least her room didn't make her barf.

Janey handed Lori the empty tape case. "Here, titles are on the back."

Even their tastes in music were different. How many years passed since Lori'd seen her cousin? People change, but this much? When Janey first extended the invitation, Lori thought it was a great idea. See Janey, do girlie stuff, and of the utmost importance, escape from home.

Janey was going to flip the cassette over when Aunt Cindy called them to supper. Lori sighed, relieved to escape this prissy room.

"You can sit there, Abi, across from Janey. What kind of pizza do you want?" Aunt Cindy asked.

Somehow, when her aunt used the shortened form of her first name didn't make her cringe like when Uncle Gary did. If not for him, she might go by Abi. "Can I have a slice of both, please?"

"Yes, you may. And drink? We have pop or milk."

Pop was a rare treat at home. The choices were milk, water or juice. "Pop, please."

"Janey, can you grab three pops out of the fridge?"

Lori took the plates from her aunt and placed them on the table.

The room was hushed except for the crunching of crust or cutlery against plates.

"How would you like to spend your time here? There are plenty of fun things to do in Regina."

"I don't know."

"That's okay. You're tired. We won't decide tonight. You sleep on it, and we can talk about it over breakfast."

Lori smiled.

"Do you want to take your pizza in the living room? I rented two movies, and we can view one while we eat."

Watch television while eating? That was unheard of at Lori's home, where they ate meals at the kitchen table.

"What ones did you rent, Mom?"

"*Can't Buy Me Love* and *Overboard*."

"Which one do you want, Ab?" Janey asked.

"Doesn't matter. I'll go along with what you two want."

They carried their plates and drinks to the other room. Lori and Janey made themselves comfortable on the floor at the oval table. After she started the movie, Aunt Cindy sat in the chair at the side of the room by the window.

Later that night, when the girls were getting into their pyjamas, Lori realized how thin her cousin had become. Her ribs stuck out, and a fine layer of long hair covered her skin. It hadn't been so noticeable with the baggy hoodie Janey had worn earlier. The girl didn't appear uncomfortable about her appearance because she didn't rush to cover her nakedness.

Lori removed one thing at a time, and replaced it with a piece of nightwear. Despite her pyjama top being long-sleeved, she didn't take off the bracelets that concealed her wrists. Those scars had to stay hidden.

Soon after she turned eleven, her self-harming started. By then, she had semi-regular periods, which enabled her to keep her uncle at bay most of the time. However, the damage had been done, and her self-esteem had shattered.

When she returned from the bathroom, a pink — of course, it was pink — teddy bear sat on the bed. She swore it wasn't there earlier. An identical one nestled against the pillows in her room at home. Lori couldn't stand to look at the stuffed animal. "Where did you get the stuffie?"

"My father. Why?"

"Um … I-I have one just like it."

"Did your father buy it for you?" Janey stopped turning back the covers and faced her cousin.

"No. Your father did."

Janey's colour drained from her face.

That was all the confirmation Lori needed.

Eight

The Scott Family Home, Ottawa, Ontario

Aug 2015

Christopher was back in his hometown for a month. He had completed the paperwork to settle his father's estate. It was now in the hands of the powers that be. He hated leaving his mother behind in that house by herself. On more than one night since his father died, he heard her crying in the bedroom his parents once shared. The longer he stayed, the harder it would be for both of them when he returned to his home in Fort McMurray.

Packing up his belongings and loading his truck reminded Chris of the first time he left this house, bound for the west. He was unwilling to stay in Ottawa one more minute. Without Marianne, he had no reason to stay. This time, the circumstances were different, making leaving much more difficult.

"Are you sure you must leave, Christopher?" His mother asked when she stopped by his bedroom door.

"Yes, Ma. I can't do anymore here. Time I made tracks for

home."

She took a tissue out of her sweater pocket and wrung it in her hands. "I wish you weren't leaving. I'll be so lonely here by myself." Mrs. Scott broke down.

Chris hugged her. "After you had all us kids under your feet, you're right. It's just been you and me since everyone headed home after Dad's funeral."

"I appreciate everything you accomplished. You did more than your share's worth, I can tell you. I don't know what I'll do without your father." She dropped on the bed.

He couldn't leave his mother in this state. His parents hadn't raised him that way. "Ma, why don't you come to Fort Mac with me for a while? I'm sure Mrs. Knowlan will watch the house, water your plants, and bring in the mail. You would be company for me on the drive. And when you're ready to return to Ottawa, I can put you on a plane or something."

"I couldn't do that."

"And why not?"

"I can't leave the house. Your father …."

"He isn't here anymore. Start living *your* life. I mean, look at all those years you couldn't talk about Evie. That wasn't right."

"I don't know."

"Sell up and move into an apartment, if your memories are what's holding you back. Construction firms are building flats in secure buildings all over the city. Elevators and everything all on one level, so you're not climbing those stairs. Make your own memories from now on. Don't erase the ones with Dad. Make a fresh start."

Her son might be onto something. The house was too much for one person. What would the other children think? They grew up in this house, in this neighbourhood. Before making decisions of that magnitude, she would discuss the matter with the others. If they all agreed she should, then Mrs. Scott would consider selling and buying a condo or renting an apartment. There were many shared memories here in their home on Elm Street. She'd spent most of her married life raising children and being a stay-at-home mother. Perhaps it was time to spread her wings? Do something for herself.

"Ma?"

Christopher's voice startled her. "Sorry, miles away."

"I gathered that. You okay?"

"Yes, yes, I'm fine. You have given me some ideas to consider, starting with going out west with you. I'd like that. Let me speak with Pat next door about watching this place, watering the plants and bringing in the mail."

"We don't need to go today, Ma. We can go tomorrow."

Christopher's suggestion of waiting until the next day to leave fell on deaf ears. His mother was already out of the house. He thought their neighbour would help. She was almost a second mother to the Scott siblings and a support for his mother during his father's last days.

It was a long journey from Ottawa to Fort McMurray, and having someone along for company would make the trip seem shorter. It took forty hours driving time, but that was with ideal roads and weather. Construction or accidents added to the duration of the drive.

Chris unpacked a few articles of clothing and his shaving kit for the morning. When his mother returned from the neighbour's, she would have to pack and then phone each of his siblings and tell them what she was doing. He couldn't begrudge her that. And wouldn't.

The solid oak door squeaked open and closed again with the click of the deadbolt. Chris would miss that sound. He'd cursed it when he was younger, trying to sneak into the house after being out until all hours. Footfalls sounded on the stairs. That one, halfway up, creaked when stepped on.

He glanced out into the hall as his mother rounded the top of the staircase. "Pat thinks it's a wonderful idea that I get away for a while. She's happy to look after the place while I'm away."

"That's fantastic, Ma."

The woman was never Pat when they were growing up. She was always Mrs. Knowlan, and she always baked the best cookies, after his mother's, and her Halloween candy — homemade popcorn balls and caramel apples. If they came from her house, they were always safe. No razor blades or straight pins or drugs in them. His mouth watered at the memory of those tasty treats.

After a simple supper of leftovers, Mrs. Scott began the arduous task of speaking to her children about the prospect of selling the family home. She was still warming casseroles from well-meaning neighbours since her husband's death. She wouldn't be able to call Michael until the following day.

Tonight, she would phone the ones still in Canada. The first one she phoned was Amy, Michael's twin.

"Hello, Amy," she said when her daughter picked up.

"Hi, Mom. What's wrong? Are you okay? You don't reach out unless you have a problem."

"Everything is fine. Christopher asked me to go to Fort McMurray with him."

"Are you?"

"Yes. Once I speak with you and your brothers and sister, I'll pack, so I'm ready when he wants to leave."

"There's more, though, isn't there."

"I carved nothing in stone, but I am thinking about it."

"About what?"

"Selling up and moving into a condo. The house is too big for one person."

After a pause, Amy said, "I think that's a wonderful idea."

Mrs. Scott chatted with her oldest daughter longer. "Well, I must go. I still have to talk to Roger and Melissa tonight. I'll have to wait and call Michael in the morning or stay awake until all hours here, so I reach him at a decent hour."

"Michael couldn't pass up the opportunity. It was too good. Yes, he's halfway around the world, but he's happy. I'll let you go so you can phone Rog and Mel. Bye, Mom. Love you."

"Love you, too. Bye."

Two of her children were in favour. Would the other three? The clock on the mantle chimed eight o'clock. Roger would be getting Adam ready for bed, so she would call Melissa first.

Melissa had just returned from taking her dachshund, Buddy, for a walk when her pocket vibrated. She pulled out her cell phone. The display read MOM. "Hi, Mom. What's up?"

"Your sister asked me the same thing when I called her."

"So there is something up. You're okay? Nothing wrong?"

"I'm fine. I'm going to Fort McMurray with Christopher. We're leaving in the morning. I'm going to stay with him for a few weeks. Maybe longer."

"What about the house? Who's going to take care of it?"

"Pat, from next door. I talked to her, and she thinks me getting away for a while is the best medicine."

"Oh, okay." The dejection in Melissa's voice came through louder than she had planned.

"There is another thing about the house. It won't be for some time. Not before I come home from your brother's. Maybe not even then, but I'm thinking about selling the house and moving into an apartment."

"What? No, you can't do that," Melissa said in a loud and high-pitched voice. "That's where we grew up."

"I thought you'd be the most difficult to persuade. Christopher and Amy are in favour."

"You might know, he would be. He's likely the one who put you up to it."

"No one is putting me up to anything I don't want."

"Like Dad forbade you to talk about Evie all these years." The words were spoken before she could take them back. "I'm sorry, Mom. I shouldn't have said that."

"You're right. What your father did was wrong. Still, the house is too much for just me."

"But where will we stay when we visit if you're not in the house anymore? I won't be able to use my old bedroom."

"Now, you're just being selfish. At least give it some thought. I'm not putting the house on the market tomorrow, and I won't do it without all my children agreeing."

Guilt hit Melissa like a punch in the stomach, only thinking about herself. The family dynamic had changed. It started with her oldest brother's girlfriend's murder in a random act of violence. Michael went off to University in Manchester and then didn't return. Amy moved away at the same time. Now her father was gone.

"I'm sorry, Mom."

"You're forgiven. I must go. I must phone Roger, but wanted to wait until after he got Adam into bed. Bye, Melissa."

"Bye, Mom." Melissa pressed the disconnect button and tried to choke back tears. If her mother sold the house, there would be no going back. Nowhere to call home in Ottawa ever again. Selfish or not, she hated the idea and knew it was Christopher who put the bug in her mother's ear.

It was a brief conversation with Roger. She had called him right in the middle of settling Adam for the night. The boy didn't have school the next day, so his father allowed him to stay up later. Her son seemed to cope well after his wife's sudden death. It lingered in the not-so-distant past and showed in his eyes.

Despite not speaking long with her second oldest, Mrs. Scott told him about going to spend some time at Chris's house in Fort McMurray. Like Amy and Melissa, he thought it was a wonderful plan. He liked the concept of her selling their family home and moving into a flat when the time came.

Michael was also in favour of her downsizing, if and when the time came. She pulled him out of the shower to answer his phone, so she didn't speak too long with him.

Nine

Janey's childhood home, Regina, Saskatchewan

Late-July 1988

The two weeks Lori stayed in Regina sped by faster than she wanted. She and Janey spent time in the park near the apartment. They hung out with her cousin's friends and went shopping with them. Her aunt even took the girls to a Roughriders football game. That was so much fun. The stands were awash with fans dressed in green and white jerseys, but even funnier were the number of people who wore hollowed out watermelons as helmets. Best of all, Saskatchewan won. Lori packed the souvenir pennant she bought at the stadium so it wouldn't get damaged when she shoved her other things into her bag.

She dreaded going home, but she had no say in the matter. Tomorrow, her relatives would see her off at the bus station, and she would be back in Yorkton at the mercy of her uncle and his whims.

It would be too late if she didn't bring it up now, especially after confirming with her cousin that she, too, was abused by Gary McNeil.

While the girls set the table, Lori worked up the nerve to ask. "Aunt Cindy, can I ask you something?"

"Of course, Abi."

"Why did you and Uncle Gary split up? I think I know. Is it what he did to Janey?"

Her aunt dropped the wooden spoon she was using to stir the spaghetti sauce and the red liquid sprayed over everything when the utensil hit the floor.

"Y-yes. Why do you ask?"

Lori shrugged.

"My God, he's abused you, too?"

"Still is when he gets the chance. I tried to tell mom, and she didn't believe me."

"I'm not putting you on that bus tomorrow. We're taking you back to Yorkton ourselves, and I'm getting to the bottom of it. Gary swore to me he stopped."

The following day, Cindy bustled around the apartment. She'd had a restless night after the bomb dropped by her niece. Her husband confessed, when she confronted him about abusing Janey. He said he had done it in the past but quit before she reached puberty. Hah! Stopped. What a liar! And now to think he's been molesting his sister's daughter. Why didn't she tell Sue and Robert straight away why she kicked Gary to the curb? Mind you, that was the last place she figured he would go.

"I called your mom and dad and told them you weren't coming on the bus. That I was bringing you home instead."

"What did they say?"

"Asked what happened. I said it was better discussed in person."

"I didn't mean to cause any trouble," Lori said as she scrambled into the backseat of her aunt's compact Chevy.

"You didn't. I should have warned your parents about him, but I didn't think Gary would go to your house. I thought he moved farther away than Yorkton. I had no clue, not that I cared, where he was until you told me he lived at your house. Since the day I kicked him out, I haven't heard a word. I might have known better with you and Janey being the same age."

"It's not your fault, Aunt Cindy. You did nothing to us."

"I know, but it doesn't make me feel any better knowing that he abused both of you. Come on. Let's get you home. Seatbelts, girls."

The closer to Yorkton they got, the more nervous Lori became. They'd passed through Melville and were about half an hour from her house. From here, the railway ran parallel to the highway. Sometimes close enough to the road, the trains were visible.

Lori's father's pickup truck was in the driveway, when Cindy pulled her car in. Would things be different if she told him what Gary had done to her? Would he have believed her? It was just a gigantic mess.

Mrs. Brownell came out to the front porch, followed by her husband. So far, no sign of Uncle Gary. Lori sighed and leapt out of the car.

As they climbed out, Lori's mother said, "I hope she's not been any trouble."

"None. I thought the drive would be nice, and since Gary is here, I decided I'd kill two birds with one stone and tell him I've filed for divorce."

"Best come in then."

Lori's father hugged her when she reached the step. "Good to have you home. The place was empty without you."

"Thanks, Dad."

"Come upstairs to my room," Lori said. "We'll find something to do so we won't be bored."

"Sure."

Lori led the way, and her cousin bounded up the stairs behind her. Ricky covered his door, across the hall from hers, in 'do not enter' signs and radioactive symbols. She smiled and shook her head. Her brother was a pain, but she missed him when he wasn't around. Missed his tormenting her.

She opened the door to her room. There it was in all its grey glory, except for the posters on her walls and the sloped part of the ceiling — Bon Jovi, Def Leppard, Journey, Queen, Pink Floyd. No flowers here. Just the way she liked it. Janey was the only one other than those who lived here who had entered her inner sanctum. Compared to her cousin's room, this was shabby. The area rug showed wear in spots, and the hardwood floor needed refinishing. Lori didn't mind. The floor's surface was as familiar to her as the back of her hand — which boards creaked when you stepped on them.

Lori removed the football pennant from her bag, then tossed the latter in the corner. She placed the souvenir along the side of the mirror on her dresser.

The sound of shattering glass echoed through the house. Now what?

"Come on. We'll see what's going on," Lori said to Janey.

They crept out of the room and down the stairs.

"Oh my God, oh my God," Mrs. Brownell wailed. "I can't believe it. My brother. And after we let him stay with us."

"Looks like Mom told them about my dad," Janey said as she huddled on the stair tread beside her cousin. Lori had chosen a spot where they couldn't be seen.

The girls held hands and waited for the other shoe to fall.

Ten

Lori's apartment, Calgary, Alberta

May 5, 2016

The situation in Fort McMurray grew more grim each day. Lori became obsessed with it. Between clients, she watched the news reports on the branch's television. The computer in her office didn't have internet access or speakers, so the TV and her mobile phone were her only way to follow the tragedy.

On one of these breaks, standing in her doorway, the scared and filthy dog wandered into the range of the camera. Someone tried to approach the animal, and it darted away. The poor thing — he was terrified. She hoped somebody caught him soon and got him out of there. How could the owner leave and not take their pet with them?

Lori left work at lunchtime intending to find a restaurant with the volume up on the television so there was audio and video. But, she didn't find a place within walking distance of the bank that would allow her to return before her lunch break ended.

All afternoon, she fretted about the animal. Another news clip played and in this one, the dog stood about fifty yards from the first location. Lori couldn't sit back and do nothing. Not to mention, she couldn't bear to see it alone in the inferno.

When Lori returned to her apartment that night, she first grabbed her laptop and searched for animal rescues after turning on the TV. A group had formed in Edmonton but was already en route to Fort McMurray. With or without help, she would rescue the male Great Dane.

She gathered blankets and pillows, filled water bottles, and packed food. Stuffed changes of clothes in a backpack. She had nothing to use as a leash, but she hoped to entice him with a tasty treat. Lori emailed her supervisor and advised her she had a family emergency and wasn't sure when she could return to work, before shutting down her computer. Despite never speaking of the dysfunctional group at work, she had one.

A quick trip to her storage locker in the basement next to the parking garage resulted in her finding some soft-sided coolers. They weren't huge, but they would do the trick. Rather than spend money on ice, she placed some bottles she'd filled earlier in the freezer. They'd help keep things from spoiling, and she and the Great Dane (if she rescued him) could drink from them once the other water ran out.

Lori set her alarm clock for five o'clock and got ready for bed. Tomorrow would be a long day. She would need plenty of rest before heading north to Fort McMurray.

Eleven

Ottawa, Ontario

Dec 31, 1999

Christopher picked Marianne up after her shift as a nurse at the Ottawa Civic Hospital. His vehicle wasn't much, but he paid off the loan, and it got him from point A to point B. That was all that mattered. He would buy something better one day.

She stood inside the entrance, and as he pulled in, she stepped out. Light snow fell, and the ground wore the beginnings of a white coat, but the streets remained wet because the flakes melted when they hit the asphalt.

With their shifts not aligning from the time Chris started his new job in Kanata, time spent with each other was a rarity. So today was one of the few times since before the tech giant hired him they were together, aside from Christmas Day.

"Hi," Marianne said as she climbed into the passenger seat.

"Have a good day?" He leaned over and kissed her. She smelled of pHisoderm and disinfectant.

"No. I'm dead on my feet. I want to go home and crash."

Those words were the last ones he wanted to hear.

"I've got to go downtown, but I'll drop you there after that. Okay?"

"All right, then." The tone of her voice showed her displeasure.

About fifteen minutes later, Christopher pulled into the underground parking lot at the Rideau Centre.

"Really? After I told you I wanted to go home, you dragged me here. You don't listen very well," she complained.

He opened her door. "You're not making it easy for me to spend time with you."

She unbuckled her seatbelt and got out. Before closing the door, Christopher wrapped his arms around her and kissed her lips, long and hard. Marianne responded to his touch and leaned into his muscular body.

Christopher took her hand, and walked her to the elevator, when they broke the embrace.

"You couldn't drop me at home, then come here?"

"It's something that requires both of us. That's all I'm going to tell you."

Maybe she was too hard on Christopher. It was the first time since Christmas Day they spent time together. He acted rather peculiar, like he was up to something, but she was so tired she couldn't figure it out. She was thinking about herself. "Will you tell me why we're here?"

"Nope."

"You're just going to drag me around a mall on New Year's Eve."

"Yup."

"Not even a hint?"

"Never."

Marianne slapped his arm and then rested her head against it. Her second wind had kicked in, and she no longer felt like a zombie.

The way Chris behaved now reminded her of their first date. They started going out together when he was in grade twelve. She was a year behind him. He didn't tell her his plans, but took her to the theatre where they saw *Mrs. Doubtfire.* Such fun that night.

Other than tonight being December 31st, 1999, it was the eve of the millennium. The world would end according to the book of Revelations, and Y2K bugs would render computers useless. Nothing significant in their conjoined lives.

A sound like a firecracker or a car backfiring echoed through the mall. A sudden burning pain formed in her torso below her left breast. She grew woozy and released her grip on Christopher's hand, and collapsed.

Two sharp pops rang out, followed by people screaming and running helter-skelter throughout the corridors. Store employees yanked their doors closed. What the …?

Marianne's fingers slipped out of his hand. Christopher turned to his right. She vanished. He dropped his gaze to the floor, where she sprawled. He fell to his knees and stroked her forehead. A red stain spread on the front of her scrubs top. Another on the tiles beneath her. Not a firecracker. Somebody in here had a gun.

Chris pulled her up to his chest. "Hang on. You're going to be okay," he whispered. She had to be. There was so much blood. He was never religious, but at this moment, he prayed for her to survive. "Someone call an ambulance," he yelled. Tears welled up in his eyes. Marianne couldn't die. Not like this. They were supposed to grow old together.

A security guard paused long enough to say police were on their way.

"My girlfriend needs medical help. Police can't do that."

"Please, sir, get into a store."

"I'm not leaving her," he snapped, and turned to his girlfriend. "I won't leave you, I swear."

She reached toward his face, but her hand dropped. Marianne died in his arms.

Why didn't he pick up the engagement ring beforehand? Had it with him in the car when he collected her from the hospital? If so, they wouldn't have been here. She wouldn't be dead. But, no. He had to do it this way. He planned to take her into the jewellery store, get down on one knee, and propose. Instead, he buried his face in her long, auburn hair and wept.

Twelve

Lori's apartment, Calgary, Alberta

May 6, 2016

The alarm clock's shrill beeping rousted Lori out of a sound sleep. She showered, dressed in jeans and a T-shirt, but pulled on a zip closure hoodie to cover her arms. Her white sneakers were on the boot tray inside the apartment door. She slipped her feet into them before heading to the underground parking, where she kept her Mini Cooper. Three trips later everything she packed from her apartment was loaded into her compact car.

Lori couldn't afford a GPS when she bought the vehicle, which she was still making payments on, so she had to rely on Google maps. Using her phone, she punched in her address and destination and set the display on the directions. In ideal conditions, it was an eight-hour journey with no guarantee the authorities would let her in. She wouldn't need the device again, except around Edmonton.

When she left Calgary, she tuned the radio to her favourite station that played music ranging from modern to the 1970s and 80s and sang along. Lori cranked up the volume when *Bohemian Rhapsody* by Queen came on.

Edmonton was about the halfway point. Lori pulled off the highway at a gas bar with a fast-food outlet attached to it and she hoped clean washrooms. She filled her Mini and, after paying, headed through to the bathrooms. An unpleasant, yet familiar, scent wafted up her nostrils when she exited the bathroom. No way. Not him? Lori froze. Cold sweat formed at the base of her skull and dripped down her back. She clawed at her wrists, peered around the doorframe, and then bolted for her vehicle as the redolence grew fainter.

Back in her car, Lori grabbed a sandwich and a bottle of water from a cooler. She pulled away because the line at the pumps was getting longer. A news flash had interrupted the music she had listened to up to this point. The fire had destroyed more homes. The beast, as people referred to the blaze, was picking up speed and strength as it tore through the city.

The dashboard clock read five when she approached a roadblock south of Fort Mac. Abandoned vehicles littered the southbound lanes and highway median. The sky was dark as night except for the eerie red glow.

"I'm part of the animal rescue group," Lori lied to the police officer. "We got separated when I got lost."

"You can't go in there. That fire is a beast. It's changed directions so many times already. There's no place where you will be safe."

"But I have to," Lori pleaded. The Great Dane loped out of the trees.

"Right there. That dog. At least let me try to rescue him."

"Five minutes. If you don't get the dog, you head south."

"Okay."

Lori leaped out of the Mini. She grabbed a plastic container, food and water from the cooler in the back. She squatted and poured cold water into the dish she had placed on the ground. "Come here, big guy. Have a drink. I bet you're thirsty."

The Great Dane stared at her but didn't run off.

"Something to eat?" Lori unwrapped a piece of beef jerky and held it out in front of her. That got his attention. He sniffed the air and took a few tentative steps toward her. "Come on, sweetheart. Come and get it." She dipped her fingers in the water and splashed it inside the bowl.

Tags dangled from the dog's collar. Was one a name tag? She could notify the owner if it was true. But she needed to catch him first.

A few more tentative steps. The dog was very close to her, but she didn't touch him. She feared he'd take off if she tried so, she continued to speak in soft tones to him. It worked, and he came closer. Lori sat on the ground beside the dish. She splashed the water again and poured some more from the bottle into it. The dog drank. She whisked his side, and he jumped but didn't run away.

"Sorry. Didn't mean to frighten you."

The Great Dane drank some more. He didn't close his mouth, and water dripped on Lori's lap, when he raised his head.

In the meantime, the police officer observed the pair. Lori knew if she didn't soon gain the dog's trust and bundle him into the car, she'd have to leave him behind, and that was not an option. She let him sniff by holding her hand with the back facing towards him. Then she turned her hand over and cupped it around his muzzle. He leaned into her touch.

Success! Lori fist-pumped and worked her fingers around the collar. One tag was his town tag, one was his rabies, and the other was his name — Wolfgang. No owner information on reverse. Contacting the city was useless because no one remained.

As she walked the dog to the Mini, one of the news agencies was doing a live feed from the scene. She was putting Wolfgang in the backseat when the police officer approached her car.

"Well done. I've seen that big guy many times, and he's always taken off until tonight. He must trust you."

"Thank you."

"Do you know of any dog-friendly places I can spend the

night?"

"No, but I think most establishments are making exceptions these days."

Lori opened the driver's door and slid in behind the wheel. "Where can I turn around?"

The police officer pointed out a driveway to her and closed the door.

"Pew. You stink," she said to the dog. "Your name should be Pepé. However, you don't smell foul like skunk, just wildfire smoke. We'll have to find you a doggie wash. Make you smell nice."

Wolfgang paid no attention. He stretched out across the seat until the car moved. Then he sat up with his head in the path of Lori's rear-view mirror.

At the first southbound rest area, Lori pulled off the road. Exhaustion washed over her and she needed to sleep. She had dozed off and snapped out of it just in time to pull the vehicle back on the pavement.

Lori parked close to the washroom building and, not having a leash for Wolfgang, took off her belt, put it around his collar, and fastened the buckle. Once he had done his business, she took him into the ladies' room with her.

The Mini was small, but she could move her seat back and recline it enough to curl up and not hit the steering wheel. Wolfgang took advantage and used the headrest for his chin.

Thirteen

Ottawa, Ontario to Beacon Hill, Fort McMurray, Alberta

Aug 2015

Christopher loaded the last of his luggage and his mother's suitcase into the rear seat of his pickup. While not designed for comfort, the extra space made an excellent place to stow things and for his dog. He had purchased the vehicle pre-Wolfgang, but he was glad he had bought the Dodge Ram Quad Cab. The manufacturer wasn't the driving force in the purchase, but the body style was. This one had the best price.

The Connollys had taken in the Great Dane when Chris made the trip east before his father's death. By now, they were likely ready to be rid of him.

He'd texted Frank the night before and told him he was returning to Beacon Hill today. It could be a much longer drive with his mother joining him. He only stopped a few times a day when he came home. Fill the tank, toilet, eat, sleep and drive some more. He pulled into a rest area and grabbed a couple of hours of nap time, if tired.

Mrs. Scott stood on Pat Knowlan's front step. She'd gone over to give the neighbour the house key. Chris felt like a voyeur as he watched the exchange on the porch. His mother turned and walked towards the truck. He had the door open and helped her up into the cab.

"Ready, Ma?"

"Yes." Her eyes were glassy with tears.

It could be a long drive.

"How did everyone take the idea of you moving into an apartment?"

"Amy was happy. So were the boys, although my timing with my calls to both of them was terrible. I caught Roger getting Adam settled for the night. And Michael? He was in the shower when I called."

"I can see him, towel wrapped around his waist, dripping on the floor. You'd have strung him up for doing that if he were at home, as in our Elm Street house," Chris said, chuckling. "You didn't mention Mel."

"She's against it. She doesn't want me to sell — says it won't be home if I'm in an apartment. And she won't be able to sleep in her old room."

"She'll get over it."

"I hope so. I don't want to upset any of you."

The trip home to Fort McMurray took longer than his trip to Ottawa, as he suspected. Not that it was a bad thing. He had slept in a bed, rather than just a few hours stolen at random rest stops and driving far too long between naps.

Four days after beginning the trip from Ottawa, Chris pulled into his driveway in Beacon Hill. He sighed, relieved to be home.

"This is your house?" Mrs. Scott asked.

"Yes, Ma."

"And you're the only one living in it?"

"It isn't just me."

His mother gave him a look that, as a child, he called the Spanish Inquisition stare. Her eyes pierced through him under an arched eyebrow. "Is there something you're not telling me? And why didn't you bring her home with you?"

"It's not like that, Ma."

"What is it like, then?"

Chris turned around. Frank, holding Wolfgang's leash, and Olivia, holding Hannah's and Becky's hands — one girl on each side — walked towards them.

"Welcome back, stranger," he said.

"Good to be home."

Chris introduced his neighbours to his mother then said to her, "Wolfgang is my roommate, Ma. He's mine. Frank and his family look after him when I'm on my two-week rotation. The girls love him, don't you, Hannah, Becky?"

"I loves Woofie," answered Becky.

Chris put his hand on her head. "I know you do. I do, too."

"You folks must be exhausted and hungry after your long journey. Why don't you join us for supper? Say about five-thirty?" Olivia asked.

"What do you say, Ma?"

After deliberating, she said. "Well, if it's not too much trouble."

"Yay! Can Woofie come, too?"

"Yes, Woofie can come, too," Frank said.

Mrs. Scott stared at the house. She realized her son had bought such an extravagant place because he intended to marry someone and start a family. The question remained, had he already picked out his future bride?

Chris grabbed the luggage out of the truck and unlocked the leaded glass door of his house. "Come on, Ma. I'll give you the grand tour."

Ceramic tile covered the foyer floor. The living room, complete with a gas fireplace, was pale hardwood boards but broader than the ones in the Elm Street house. Under the large window sat a leather sofa. A bookcase in the corner held an assortment of CDs and DVDs. Two speakers straddled the fireplace, stretching almost to the height of the mantle. His TV and stereo equipment sat on a low stand across the room from the sofa. A leather La-Z-Boy was next to the fireplace.

Exercise equipment filled the dining room — a stationary bike, a treadmill, and an elliptical, so the kitchen must be spacious enough to house a table and chairs. There was no set there either, when they reached that room. There was a peninsula and four bar stools instead. It would do for her son. The workout space would have to move when he got married.

"I'll give you the bedroom on this floor. Save you climbing the stairs. The bathroom is here." Christopher opened the door to the room.

"What's upstairs?" Mrs. Scott asked.

"An en-suite bedroom and two more bedrooms that share a bathroom."

His home was dust-free, considering the time he was away. Did Olivia come over and clean this week, knowing he would be back soon?

"Do you want to see upstairs, Ma?"

Mrs. Scott started for the staircase.

"Do you want a cup of tea? Sorry, I don't have any milk. I sent what I had over to Frank and Olivia before I came home. Cleaned out the fridge of anything perishable."

"A glass of cold water would be lovely."

"Coming right up."

Mrs. Scott ascended the stairs. Her son's house was gorgeous. It must have cost Christopher well over half a million dollars. Yet, she didn't begrudge him owning a home. She and her late husband encouraged their children to save and buy rather than rent for the rest of their lives. Her concern, with a property this lavish, was could Christopher afford it? What if the drilling depleted the oil sands, and he lost his job? Then what?

This level of the house was immaculate, the same as it was on the main level.

When five-thirty arrived, Chris and his mother walked across the street to join his neighbours.

"We're only cooking hamburgers and hotdogs with salads," Olivia said apologetically. "We like to BBQ as often as possible when we have warm weather."

"It will be fine," Mrs. Scott said.

"Do you want a beer, Chris?" Frank asked.

"Sure, why not?"

"What about you, Mrs. Scott? Can I get you something? I think Olivia has a bottle of Chardonnay in the fridge."

"That would be lovely. And, please, call me Lucille."

"Why don't you folks make yourselves comfortable out on the deck, and I'll bring out the drinks?"

Chris led his mother to the sliding doors leading to the outdoor space. The last time he visited, Frank was still building the multi-level area. The uppermost was the cooking and eating area. Below was seating with an outdoor sectional sofa, armchairs and a propane fire table.

Wolfgang raced down the steps to the grass and frolicked with Hannah and Becky.

It was a pleasant evening. Good friends. Good food. Good company. It was almost nine-thirty when Chris, his mom and Wolfgang returned home.

Fourteen

Christopher's home, Beacon Hill, Fort McMurray, Alberta

Sept 2015

"It's time I returned to Ottawa. I've imposed on you long enough."

"Are you sure, Ma?"

"Hannah and Becky are in school. Olivia's back in her teaching position. When you're gone for two weeks at a time, I rattle around the house with the dog."

Wolfgang's ears twitched at the reference.

"Besides, how are you going to bring any lady friends back to the house with me here?"

"Ma, there are no lady friends."

"Me being here isn't helping in that department, Christopher."

"Maybe I'm not interested in having a lady friend."

"Is it related to what happened to Marianne?"

"I *have* dated since I moved out here. I just haven't found the right girl."

Mrs. Scott arched her eyebrow at him.

"All right, Ma. I'll book you on a flight back to Ottawa. Do you think Mrs. Knowlan can pick you up at the airport once you know your arrival information? Cab fare will cost you a fortune to take you from the airport to the house."

"You let me worry about that."

Chris disappeared and returned a few minutes later with a laptop. He sat on the couch with the computer on the cocktail table.

Mrs. Scott had enjoyed her time in Fort McMurray, but it was time to go home. She'd been here long enough. She cramped her son's style for too long and was unsure if she believed him about dating off and on. After all, Marianne's death had a profound effect on him. She had never seen him so broken before.

Within an hour, Chris had his mother booked on a flight from Fort McMurray to Ottawa with a stop in Calgary. The one he chose worked the best for when she would arrive back in Ottawa.

"Your flight leaves the day after tomorrow around seven o'clock, so we'll have to be at the airport no later than five to get you through check-in and security."

"That's fine. I'm an early riser, and we'll go to bed earlier tomorrow night if needs must."

The woman was practical; he would give her that. It was time for them to part company after having her for a visit. She hadn't cried since she came to Fort Mac with him, or it was when he was at work. But would being back in the house on Elm Street in Ottawa take her back to the day her husband died? His biggest concern about her staying in the house alone was that and the stairs.

He pulled out his cell phone and scrolled to his group chat in Messenger. One message and all the family would know the plan, rather than individual messages. That wasn't a worry when his mother came to Fort Mac. She had phoned everyone.

Putting Ma on an Air Canada the day after tomorrow.

She'll arrive in Ottawa at 4:10 pm.

Two replies popped up in Messenger. Melissa's was first, followed by Amy's. Roger's response came in later that evening, and Michael's not until the following morning.

Chris lived less than half an hour from the airport, but rather than take chances on not getting his mother to the terminal in time to catch her flight; he woke around four. It had seemed strange using the upstairs en-suite bedroom. Until his mother came to stay, he always slept in the one he gave her. He tried to move around upstairs so he didn't disturb her, but when he walked into the kitchen to make coffee, his mother was already making breakfast.

"That's not necessary."

"It's going to be a long day. I'm making sure we start out on the right foot. And that's with a hearty breakfast. Now sit."

That was him told. He poured himself a cup of medium roast and did what his mother said.

"Have you contacted Mrs. Knowlan about meeting you at the airport when you arrive in Ottawa?"

"No. I'll call her when the plane lands. I figure by the time my bags come off the plane, she'll be there. That way, Pat won't have to pay for parking. Just pull up, I'll climb in with my bags, and we're off home."

Practical and logical. He'd heard that the price of parking at the airport had skyrocketed, so saving their neighbour's parking fees, although his mother would reimburse the woman, was the thing to do.

Once they'd finished their bacon, eggs, home fries, mushrooms and toast breakfast, Chris loaded his mother's bags into his truck. At least they had wheels, so it would be easier for her to navigate with them.

At the airport, Chris made the turn for short-term parking.

"Just drop me outside the terminal. I'm a big girl. I can look after myself. You don't need to accompany me."

"You sure?"

"Yes."

Chris changed lanes and drove to the building's entrance. He helped his mother out of the passenger seat, retrieved her luggage, and extended the handles on the bags. "You've got your ticket and boarding pass I printed for you?"

"In my purse."

"You'll call me when you get home?"

"Yes, Christopher."

Chris hugged his mother goodbye and watched as she disappeared through the sliding doors, suitcase in each hand and her purse over her shoulder. He stood there until airport security approached him about moving his vehicle.

When he walked into his house, it felt right. Wolfgang met him in the foyer, wagging his tail. "Just the two of us now, Wolfie." Chris grabbed the leash from the coat tree. "Let's go for a walk."

Fifteen

Lori's childhood home, Yorkton, Saskatchewan

Late-July 1988

"I'm so sorry. I would have told you both if I knew Gary was coming to you," Cindy said. She dropped on one of the kitchen chairs and said, "I threw him out because he abused Janey."

Sue sat across from her, expressionless.

Bert paced. "When I get my hands on him …."

"He's not worth the effort. He would press assault charges on you if you laid a finger on him. You don't want that. You'd lose your job."

Lori's dad muttered something, but Cindy could not decipher it.

"My poor baby. She told me, and I didn't believe her. What kind of mother am I?" Mrs. Brownell picked a tissue out of the box. She dabbed her eyes, then twisted the Kleenex until it fell apart in her hands.

"You're a wonderful mother, Sue. A wonderful one," her husband comforted.

The backdoor slammed shut. Cindy stopped dead. She launched herself across the room at him, sending the chrome chair clattering to the floor, when Gary entered the kitchen. "Damn you, Gary, you swore you stopped! You lied to me!" She pounded her fists against his chest.

"Abigail, Janey, can you girls come down here?" Mr. Brownell shouted, then pulled Cindy away from her husband.

The girls soon appeared in the doorway.

Cindy took a deep breath and continued her verbal assault on her husband. "Your daughter is starving herself to death, thanks to you. She's anorexic. What do you think of that? Oh, and your niece? She's self-harming. It's okay, honey; it was your way of coping. I saw your scars when I took you girls to the football game, but didn't put it together until you told me that Gary was abusing you."

"I'll call the police," Bert moved to the wall-mounted phone outside the kitchen door. "They'll be here soon," he said on his return.

Lori sidled over to her mother, keeping her back to the wall to put as much distance between herself and her uncle as possible. "I'm sorry, Mom."

"It wasn't your fault. It was Gary's." She bundled her daughter into her arms and hugged her.

"Why didn't you call the police then? When you found out he was abusing Janey?"

"I don't know, Bert, I just wanted him out of my house, away from my daughter. I never dreamed he would come here."

"Wouldn't come here to his sister's house. Hard to believe. Once the police finish here, I want you and Janey out of my house."

"No, Dad. The only one who needs to leave is Uncle Gary, and the police will arrest him."

"Abigail." Her father arched his eyebrow.

The RCMP arrived. One officer took Lori to the living room, where she spoke with her about the incidents. Despite her fear, she told her what her uncle did to her. She even showed her scars from self-harming. The policewoman nodded and wrote everything down in her small notebook. "You and your parents must come to the detachment to swear out a full statement. You have nothing to be afraid of. Just tell them what you've told me here today, and then you'll sign it. Your parents can be with you. We'll have to speak with them, too. Will it be okay to do that? Oh, and we'll need to take pictures of your arms."

Lori nodded to the kind woman. Having the whole ugly situation out in the open felt good. Whether she could stop self-harming was another story. Stressful situations made her do that, and during the interview, her fingers scratched at her wrists.

The police led Uncle Gary away in handcuffs. She and Janey clung to each other as they took him out. He couldn't hurt either of them as long as he was in jail. Lori hoped he'd rot there and thought her cousin might feel the same way.

Sixteen

Lori's childhood home, Yorkton, Saskatchewan

May 7, 2016

"Bert, come in here. Quick! It's Abigail," Sue Brownell called to her husband. She had the small television in the kitchen tuned to the news while she cooked breakfast.

Her husband came into the room, razor in hand and half of his face covered in shaving cream. "What is it?"

"Look, there. Abigail. I'd recognize her walk anywhere. No one else I know of walks with a limp like that."

He peered at the small screen. "Turn the volume up. I want to hear what they're saying."

Sue picked up the remote and adjusted the volume.

"... and out of all this gloom and destruction comes a heartwarming tale. Just behind me, a dog roaming the streets since city officials ordered the mandatory evacuation is being rescued. We've spotted him many times in the past three days, but until today, no one has got near him."

"Is this live?"

"No. This is from late yesterday. Abigail was in Fort

McMurray yesterday. She's safe, thank heavens."

Smoke filled the kitchen.

"Sue, the bacon."

The smoke detector went off. Its shrill noise pierced the relative quiet of the small storey and a-half home. Mrs. Brownell grabbed the lid, placed it on the frypan, and turned the element off. The grease hadn't caught fire, but it smoked. Sue opened the window to let the smoke out.

Safe. And at least for a while, her daughter was in Fort Mac. Abigail vanished after starting her post-secondary education at Lakeland College in Lloydminster, Alberta. Sue sighed with relief. She had worried and thought the worst. Half expected the police to show up at the house or Tim Hortons with news they'd found Abigail's body.

Guilt plagued her, too, since she didn't believe her daughter when she said her uncle abused her. Worse still was that the culprit was Sue's brother.

Seventeen

The Scott Family home, Ottawa, Ontario

Jan 1, 2000

On New Year's Day, camera crews and reporters from newspapers and the television networks camped on Elm Street outside the Scott home. The previous night, some media people followed Chris.

Marianne's parents met the police and ambulance at the hospital. The way her mother glared at him. He had to come to grips with the fact she thought of him as something she had scraped off the bottom of her shoe. "I was picking up her engagement ring. I was going to ask her to marry me on the spot." His explanation after the fact sounded feeble, even to him.

He had been in no condition to drive. He would have wrapped his little beater around a telephone pole to eliminate his pain. His appearance must have given him away, because one of the investigating officers offered to drive him home.

Chris stood in the front room window, peering around the sheer curtains that covered it from ceiling to floor.

"Where's your car, Chris?" Melissa asked.

"At the mall," he said. Right away he felt guilty for snapping at her. She had done nothing to deserve his anger and frustration.

His sister's eyes welled up. He'd hurt her feelings.

"I'm sorry. I shouldn't take it out on you. What happened isn't your fault."

"Were you going to ask Marianne to marry you?"

"Yup."

"I'm sorry. I liked her." Melissa slipped her hand into his.

"And she liked you." Chris drew in a ragged breath. His eyes teared up again. One escaped, and he dashed it away before his little sister saw him crying. Real men were stronger than that. They didn't show their emotions. But he couldn't help himself. How would he survive the next few days? Weeks? Months? Years without Marianne at his side?

"Whenever you want to go pick up your car, son," Mr. Scott said as he entered the room. "I see, that lot is still there. They haven't got the decency to let a family grieve. I can't imagine the number of vultures over at the Lawson's."

Chris shouldered his way past his father. "Sorry, Dad." He took the stairs two at a time until he reached his bedroom and slammed the door. He leaned back against it and scrubbed his hands down his face.

"I didn't mean to make Chris upset," Melissa said.

"I know, sweetie, but I didn't help things either by mentioning picking up his car." Mr. Scott placed his hand on Melissa's head.

She wrapped her arms around her father's waist and rested her head against his chest. "Will we attend the wake and funeral?"

"Your mother and I will. However, I don't expect the Lawsons will appreciate our entire family landing in on them."

"Not even Chris?"

"We'll go with Chris or meet him there or whatever he needs us to do."

"I liked Marianne."

"We all did."

"I want to go."

"We'll see, sweetie." Mr. Scott pried himself out of Melissa's arms and turned towards the kitchen.

She sat on the arm of the chair and watched the newspeople outside the house. A fistfight almost broke out between two camera operators, jostling for the prime position. Melissa giggled. They were recording again. A reporter stood facing away from the house on the sidewalk. She jumped back from the window to remain unseen.

"I'm going out, Ma. I can't stay in here and do nothing," Chris said.

"Go out the back way. I can't bear that lot swarming you as soon as you're out the door."

Chris checked out the window and then turned towards the rear of the house. He left this way many times, so his parents didn't hear him leave. The times Chris had snuck out to meet Nick and Ron, back then when they were teens, the three were holy terrors, according to his mother.

Today, he didn't care if the door closed without a sound. Not that he would slam it shut, but it was not like the old days. Once outside, Chris plotted his next move. Either way, it necessitated scaling a few fences. If he turned right, he would come out on Rochester. Straight ahead, Spruce, and to the left, Booth. He rubbed his neck while he decided.

He couldn't deal with the news people outside his house. Not today. Not ever. They couldn't bring Marianne back any more than he could. Their questions would only make him suffer more than he already was.

Escape successful, Chris wandered the streets around his home. At the corner of Booth and Elm, he paused. The media circus was enormous outside the Scott house closer to the far end of the block. From this vantage point, they were visible to him, but he wasn't to them.

Doreen Lawson yanked another tissue out of the box, dabbed her eyes and blew her nose. "Why can't they leave us to grieve?" she moaned as she twisted it around her fingers. Each hour, the horde outside their semi-detached home on Arthur Street grew larger.

"They're only doing their job," her husband, William, said. "I realize it's uncomfortable having them out there, but they'll soon get cold or bored and go away."

"Father Marcello is coming again today?" She meant it as a statement but came out as a question.

"When he left, he said he would. Here come away from the window. You're only upsetting yourself." William guided her to the dining room.

"Christopher Scott is who's got me upset. What was he thinking of taking Marianne to the Rideau Centre on New Year's Eve? Especially this one in particular. He should have known every kook in the country would proclaim the end of the world." Doreen folded her arms around her waist.

"How was he to know? No one was. It was a freak accident."

"It took our daughter's life. Our only child. It was no accident, William. It was deliberate."

The doorbell rang, putting an end to their conversation. Mr. Lawson left her side to greet their visitor.

"Tell them to go away." She moved into the hallway.

Father Marcello squeezed his bulky frame through the open door. Reporters aimed microphones towards it, camera flashes going off, and the cacophony of voices asking for a few words — a media circus.

"I'm sorry about all that. They followed me when they saw me coming up your steps."

They wouldn't leave until they got what they came for. An interview with the grieving. The priest led Doreen to the dining room, helped her into a chair, pulled one around, and sat facing her. She was not a devout Christian, but this man's words of sympathy and prayers calmed her. Just holding her hands helped.

"Did you contact the funeral home yet? Planned for the funeral?"

"No."

"Would you like me ...?"

"I can't believe she's gone," Doreen wailed.

William put his hand on her shoulder. "Would you, Father? My wife is not fit to do that job."

"It would be my pleasure. Any place you had in mind?"

"That place on Cooper Street. It looks like a huge red brick house," said William. "Is that okay with you, dear?"

Doreen nodded.

"And the cemetery?"

"Doreen's family has plots in the one on Prince of Wales Drive."

"The memorial gardens?"

"Yes."

"Why don't I try to get someone to come to you? That way, you don't have to fight with the media."

"Don't get up. I'll see myself out."

After the priest left, William helped his wife upstairs. "You lie down for a while. You didn't sleep a wink last night." Once he settled her, he pulled the covers over her. "I'm just downstairs if you need me," he said as he shut the door behind him.

He didn't go downstairs as he had told his wife. Instead, he shuffled to Marianne's room. William stood in the doorway. His little girl was never coming home. He was so proud of her when she graduated from nursing school with top grades. Happy for her when she got the job at the Ottawa Civic. He choked back a sob and dropped to her desk chair.

Her room was as she left it. She wouldn't be going there anymore, either. Her patients and coworkers would miss her a great deal. He and Doreen didn't mind her still living at home. She was saving for a down payment on a condo closer to her job. William did not know how close she'd gotten to her goal, but he knew she didn't spend her money frivolously.

A photo of Marianne and Chris stared at him from a glass frame on her desk. She held a giant stuffed animal. One of their friends took the picture at the Ottawa Ex last year. Christopher won the big bear. They were both smiling and happy and in love.

William was about to leave when Doreen appeared in the doorway.

"I thought I'd find you in here." She selected a small teddy bear and perched on the bed.

"I couldn't go downstairs without coming in first. Doreen, what are we going to do? I miss her so much already; it hasn't been twenty-four hours yet."

"I know. I feel the same way." She reached out her hand, and he grabbed it in both hands.

"She should be cremated, don't you think?"

"I don't want to think about that, William. It's too painful. I have enough problems knowing that some lunatic murdered our daughter, and Christopher Scott led her to her death. I can't move past that."

William sighed. Chris was not the one to blame. Until she realized otherwise, mentioning Marianne's fiancé's name would draw his wife's ire.

Chris wandered throughout the neighbourhood. The smells and sounds of the city wrapped him in their presence. Diesel fumes from the buses, exhaust odours from car engines mingled with cooking oil, frying and grilling foods from various eateries. Any other day, he would embrace it, but today was not any other day. Today, he found them oppressive. Found them suffocating.

He paused at the corner of Somerset and Arthur. On the occasions he walked to Marianne's house, he always came this way, by the Chinese market and down her street. The media scrum outside her home was larger than the one at his. They had that thoroughfare blocked.

With his mind elsewhere, he stepped off the curb. Brakes screeched, and a horn blared, but the motorist stopped in time.

The driver shook his fist as he passed. Chris didn't care if he got hit by the car. He wished they had injured him enough that he died. At least he would be reunited with Marianne.

Eighteen

South of Fort McMurray, Alberta

May 7, 2016

Lori woke with a start. Where was she? What was that foul stench? She stretched and looked around. She was in her car. It came back to her. She pulled off the road to sleep. The horrible smell emanated from Wolfgang. Dog and wildfire smoke.

After a bite to eat and drink for both of them, and a bathroom break, she resumed her southbound journey. She needed to find a doggie wash somewhere and bath the Great Dane. Thus, eliminating the odour from him. Not to mention, her car interior would also need a thorough cleaning. But then, unless she dried his coat, she would also have the wonderful wet dog aroma. It might be best to wait until she returned to Calgary. Then call a place that did auto detailing to come and clean her car. Some car washes had dog wash stations. Failing that, a pet store equipped with one.

At least Wolfgang behaved in the car. He didn't pace, pant or whine. The giant dog never tried to squeeze between the seats to get into the front. He stretched out across the back seat most of the time. Once in a while, he rested his chin on the console.

The wildfire scent of burning leaves, wood, furniture, and melted plastic brought back another memory from her past. Uncle Gary had built a bonfire in the backyard. Incensed with her, he tossed her stuffed animals into the flames. She had cried for him not to do it; that she would submit to his whims. What did she do to make him so mad? Her pleas didn't help, and the toys burned. Worst of all, he mocked her for crying.

Lori wanted to post on social media that she rescued a dog from Fort McMurray. To keep her uncle from finding her, she had locked down her account so that only her friends saw anything she wrote. In addition, the time between her posts was irregular. So how could she make it known she found the dog?

She pulled out her phone and took a picture of Wolfgang. The profile picture wasn't of her, but one of her crocheting projects. Her family didn't know her new identity, not even her cousin, who accompanied her when she changed her name. Lori took a chance, toggled from only friends to public, uploaded the photo and began her post.

FOUND in Fort McMurray. Male Great Dane named Wolfgang. If he's yours, please PM me. She took a deep breath and pushed the post button. With luck, the dog's owner, and not every idiot and his brother, would message her and they could meet and she'd return the animal.

Nineteen

Lakeland College, Lloydminster, Alberta

Sept 1993

Lori scoured the student library at Lakeland College for information on how to go about changing your name, but without success. She wanted to do it before they released her uncle from prison to ensure he couldn't find her.

She asked the librarian, and she told her it was research for an English essay. No luck. Her English teacher. He didn't know either. The professor surmised the person would need to do it in their birth province and wouldn't be free. While he was of little help, at least she had a starting point.

Despite receiving more than enough to live on in a student loan, bursaries and grants, Lori didn't wish to spend a fortune. Yet, in order for her grades to be recognized from pre-name change to post, she needed to go through the legal channels.

That night, when she should do homework, she pulled out her favourite pen and a sheet of lined paper and wrote a letter to her cousin, Janey, in Regina.

Janey,

    I need you to do me a huge favour. I want to change my name and can't find anything in the library.

Thanks.
Abigail

P.S. don't tell anyone what I'm doing. This has to be kept secret.

She addressed the envelope, enclosed the letter and sealed it. She could buy a stamp at the bookstore and mail the note. Doing this bit made her feel better. Like she was regaining control in her life.

Lori stopped at the campus bookstore and purchased her stamp before her first class. After that, she walked to the mailbox near the road and managed not to be late. She didn't trust anyone to do this for her, lest her letter go astray and her quest be unsuccessful.

She slipped into a seat near the back of the classroom seconds before the instructor closed the door. Math was her number one worst subject. With numbers, she couldn't wrap her head around some functions. English or History she breezed through them. But the Business Administration program offered math, accounting, business management, economics, marketing, strategic planning and English.

Once the right teacher came along, her stumbling blocks

fell into place and she achieved success in that troublesome subject.

She didn't know how long it would take Janey to find and send her the requested information, but she hoped to hear back from her cousin sooner than later. Lori carried her birth certificate in her wallet. She might need to have the document photocopied and notarized. She knew the person she wanted to become. No longer would she be Abigail Laurie Brownell, a mousy girl afraid of her own shadow. With her new identity, Lori would no longer shrink away into a corner. She would stand up for herself.

Two weeks later, the dorm mail person pushed an envelope under her door. A letter from Janey lay on the floor. Lori tossed her books on her bed and snatched up the piece of mail, praying for good news.

Abigail,

You won't like this. It's going to cost you over $200.00 to change your name. Because you're a victim of abuse, and with my father due to be released in 2014, there should be no problems at all. You'll have to swear out an affidavit about the abuse.

You must live in the province. So I'm not sure how that will work with you studying in Alberta.

A criminal background check has to be done within 14 days of the application.

I understand why you want to change your name. I get it, but you will not like that the folks at vital statistics advertise the name change. They might not in an abuse case. Guess you'll find that out when you do.

Same-day service is available for an additional fee. I'll go with you, if you come to Regina. Let me know. I hope school is going well.

Janey

Same-day service was appealing. The cost was nuts. Mind you; all Lori spent her loan and grant money on was food, feminine products, soap, shampoo and school supplies. She didn't go out anywhere but stayed in residence — so nothing to spend her money on. Growing her hair out might require a bit more shampoo and possibly conditioner. Lori could work out a more strict budget and stick to it.

Travelling to Regina to do the deed in person caused her to take at least one day off school because government offices weren't open on weekends. She needed a bus schedule. She had seen them on campus. In the bookstore? Once she checked and got the times, duration, and return trip information, she could get back to Janey. The sooner she did, the better. The semester or Christmas break was too late. And her luck, the office she needed would be closed then, too.

Lori found the transit schedule in the bookstore. A weekly service ran between Lloydminster, here at the campus, and Regina, not daily as she had hoped. She would have to fabricate some story to take a week off school. But she opted to go as soon as possible before her course loads got too heavy. She might not catch up if she fell behind. Maybe her instructors would provide her with the assignments she would miss and she could work on them while she was in Regina and not fall behind.

That created another problem. Accommodations. Would her aunt let her stay there? It had been a long time since she spent two weeks with Cindy and Janey. Her cousin wouldn't have a problem with it. Despite the geographic distance between them, the girls remained close. So when she wrote back with the dates and times, she asked if it was okay to stay with them.

First, she needed to go to the local RCMP detachment and start proceedings for her criminal background check. With luck, the turnaround would be quick, and she could leave the following Wednesday after her last class. It meant being on the bus overnight and arriving early in the morning, but that was okay. Lori would sacrifice a night's sleep for the cause.

It was mid-afternoon when Lori's last class of the day ended. She returned to the residence long enough to ensure she had all the paperwork before setting out for the RCMP offices.

"I need to apply for a criminal background check," she

said into the intercom.

The constable at reception behind the glass doors buzzed her in.

After she completed the paperwork, Lori said, "I have to go to Saskatchewan next week. Will this be ready by then?"

"It only takes forty-eight hours, sometimes longer." She stamped the request form RUSH. "That will ensure a quick turnaround for you. Good luck in our neighbouring province."

Lori left the police station relieved. She preferred not to reveal why she needed the background check or was going home — not quite home, but close enough. The fewer people who knew, the safer she felt. The less chance of her uncle discovering her whereabouts. He was not due for release for some time yet, thanks to the judge sentencing him to consecutive sentences rather than concurrent. Under normal circumstances, judges went with the latter when sentencing criminals, but the heinousness of Gary's crime was such the judge opted for the former.

She noticed a drugstore in the mall across the street, when she walked to the RCMP offices, so on her way home, she stopped in. Throughout high school and until now, she never wore makeup, but starting tomorrow, she would.

She selected some inexpensive eyeliner and mascara, a soft peach-coloured blush that came with a brush, a lip liner and lipstick to match the shade of the powder.

Back in her dorm room, Lori practiced with the makeup. Her first attempts were disastrous. The eyeliner made her look like a raccoon. Once she mastered that, she tried the blush again with less than stellar results. She'd applied too much and looked like a clown. Frustrated with her lack of ability to perform the simplest of tasks, she swept the cosmetics off the vanity top.

It was time to write to Janey.

Janey,

I started the process for the criminal background check today. The receptionist at the police station says it takes 48 hours, but she put a rush on it to be certain.

I'm taking the bus next Wed afternoon and will arrive in Regina around 6:30 Thursday morning. Can you believe it takes over 13 hours? And get this, when I leave the following Wed morning, the trip is less than 10 hours.

See you then.
Abigail

Lori was unwilling to tell anyone her new name, especially in a letter that could go astray. However, Janey would find out soon enough, since she offered to go with her.

Twenty

Millennium Lodge, north of Fort McMurray, Alberta

May 8, 2016

After his shift ended, Chris returned to the lodge. He grabbed a change of clothes and headed for the shower. It felt fantastic to remove sweat and dirt from the day's work, not to mention eliminate the sour scent of sweat. Even he admitted he reeked.

Chris made his way to the recreation hall and dining room after he returned his work clothes to his room. News of the fire filled the television screen. They were filming this segment in Beacon Hill. The scene behind the newscaster appeared familiar to him, but with the destruction, he couldn't tell if it was his street or not. Many of the homes on the site appeared similar to the one where his house stood. Sometimes, the only difference was the colour of the brick and the vinyl siding.

Today's supper menu was chili with nachos, or chicken and mashed potatoes and gravy with mixed vegetables. Chris chose the Mexican dish and two butter tarts for his dessert, then sat with two of the guys from his work area. One of them scrolled Facebook on his phone as he ate. "Hey, Chris. Isn't this your dog?" He turned the phone, so that Chris could read the post.

"Sure looks like my Wolfgang." He extracted his phone from his jeans pocket, opened the app, and searched for the sender's name. This was the only post from this person visible. Her privacy settings must be set to friends only, or she just opened an account. He clicked on the message button and, when Messenger opened, typed.

That sure looks like my dog. City tag, rabies tag, name tag?

Yes.

Neutered? He waited for her reply. It took longer for a response to come through.

Yes.

Things pointed to this being his missing dog. Did Wolfgang have any other distinguishing features he could mention? The three dots bounced on his screen. She was typing something.

Is your Great Dane's lower right canine chipped?

Yes! It was Wolfgang. Chris fist-pumped. "Yes!"

"Good news, I take it?"

"The best. Someone found Wolfgang, and he is safe."

"That *is* terrific news, mate."

The news excited Chris so much that he couldn't finish his meal. He finished his chili and nachos and passed the butter tarts to the men at his table. He needed to arrange with this Lori person to return Wolfgang.

Back in his room, Chris typed out another message.

I work at SUNCOR and don't get off until the 21st. I hate to ask, but can you keep Wolfgang with you until then?

He waited for a response. Then, when one didn't come back straight away, he typed another.

I'll reimburse you for his food and any other expenses you incur while Wolfie is in your care.

She might be receptive to keeping the dog longer. Chris sat the phone down and wiped the back of his neck. First, he needed to text his sister and tell her that someone found Wolfgang, but he wanted to wait for a response.

Chris wasn't the most patient person in the world, and he paced his room and checked the phone. Finally, the three dots began bouncing on the screen.

I'll keep him until you come for him. Don't worry about reimbursing me. I don't mind. It will be wonderful to have a built-in roomy and bodyguard.

What did that last statement mean? Was she in danger, or just being funny? If it was the latter, she should have used a laughing emoji or something. Her comment worried him.

He scrolled to his family group chat in his Messenger contacts and typed a quick missive.

Wolfgang rescued, and all is well.

Melissa returned his message with multiple heart emojis and a smiley.

Twenty-One

The Lawson family home, Arthur Street, Ottawa, Ontario

Jan 2, 2000

A few minutes after nine o'clock, the funeral director phoned the Lawson home.

"I won't leave here until that media circus outside our front door has gone," Doreen said to her husband.

William spoke again, "I'm sorry, she's adamant she's not leaving the house. I don't suppose you could bring the brochures and come to us? I know it's a huge thing for us to ask."

The person on the other end of the phone was talking during the pause.

"Thank you. We look forward to seeing you." After hanging up the phone, William walked into the living room. "They'll be here at eleven."

"Father Marcello is joining us, too?" she asked.

"If you'd like."

"Please."

"I'll call him then."

Doreen shuffled to the kitchen and put the kettle on to boil. Tea. A hot cup of Earl Grey in a china cup. And not a bag in a mug. Made in a real teapot and left to steep. She retrieved the pot with no issues, but when she picked up the cup on its saucer, her hand shook, sending the delicate piece of pottery to the floor. The china shattered when it hit the ceramic tile surface, and Doreen collapsed on the floor in tears.

William returned to the hall and placed the call. He could do with the priest spending less time at the house. He didn't find the man's words of any comfort, but his wife did, so he would do it as much as it behooved him.

As a shadow passed the window, William put the phone down. A woman dashed across the street. Did she leave something on their porch? He'd worry about that after he called Father Marcello.

"Yes, Father. Again. Doreen's insisting," he said. "Thank you for contacting the funeral home yesterday. The director will arrive at eleven. Perhaps you arrived before that? It will be difficult, but having you here might keep the missus from falling off the rails."

"Of course."

"Thank you. We'll see you then."

William hung up the phone. His little girl had only been gone two days. It seemed like years. Doreen was a mess. She did nothing but cry. Wouldn't eat. Didn't sleep well — not that he did either. The only time she didn't weep was when Father Marcello was in the house. He would put up with it if it was necessary to maintain some quiet.

He walked into the kitchen to advise his wife the priest was coming, too. He found her on the floor surrounded by shards of broken china teacup.

The funeral director and priest arrived together. Father Marcello handed William an envelope when he opened the door to allow them passage. "This was lying on your step," he said.

Did that woman he saw running off his porch leave that? He ushered the two men into the living room, where he had situated Doreen. Once he was on his own in the foyer, he opened the package.

Please, would you allow me to interview you and your wife regarding the tragic accident that took your daughter's life? I assure you my piece will be very sympathetic instead of the sensational drivel other media outlets publish. You can contact me on my cell at 613-555-0000 if you agree.
Joanna

Mr. Lawson crumpled the letter, tossed it and the envelope in the wastebasket and joined the others.

A few hours later, they had made the arrangements. The first viewing would be on the fourth.

Twenty-Two

Millennium Lodge, north of Fort McMurray to Edmonton, Alberta

May 16, 2016

Chris had just finished his shift and returned to the lodge when the alarm sounded announcing the work camp evacuation. Chris scooped his belongings into his duffel bag and rushed to his truck. The driver parked the bus that ferried SUNCOR employees to and from the city facing the road.

Evacuated employees couldn't go home. They locked Fort Mac down. At least, the southbound lanes remained open on the main highway so that he could leave the area. Chris was getting away. He tossed his bag into the back seat of his truck, eased behind the wheel, and started the engine. When he took off from the parking lot, gravel sprayed from under his tires.

The orange and red of the flames were visible through the haze. He needed to use the wipers on the truck to keep the windshield clear of the ash that rained down. Sometimes, the wind blew live embers in with the debris.

The drive, which only took about half an hour from the

camp to his house in Beacon Hill, took twice as long because of the poor visibility. Chris steered his Dodge Ram with caution through the city. Landmarks familiar to him had disappeared. Twisted metal was all that remained of some businesses which lined the highway.

The farther he drove away from Fort Mac, the better the visibility became. Less ash fell out of the sky. Chris continued until he reached the first rest area south of Fort McMurray. At least they did not cordon it off. He pulled in and stopped his truck about midway. He just drove through hell. Stepping out of the cab, Chris laced his fingers behind his head. From what he saw driving through the city, nothing remained. Not one structure. He would have to contact his insurance broker, but with the town in ruins, it would be difficult, if not impossible. That meant he'd have to go through the insurance company's head office. Who knew how long that would take?

Chris retrieved his phone from the cupholder and opened the Messenger app. When he found Lori on the list, he typed out a message.

Work camp evacuated. I'm south of Fort Mac in the first rest area. Where are you?

We could meet at Chateau Lake Louise by the underground parking. Say 2:00 on the 18th?

As much as Chris wanted Wolfgang back, he needed to shower, shave, do laundry, and sleep. With the evacuation, that might be an arduous task. He would drive to Edmonton tonight. Get some things done the next day. Leave for Lake Louise on the morning of the 18th.

I'm going to get to Edmonton tonight. I need to make myself presentable. See you on the 18th at 2:00.

With the arrangements now made for their rendezvous, Chris climbed back into the truck and continued his journey. He had waited this long to reunite with his dog; what were two more days?

Chris passed a few roadside motels before he reached Edmonton, but the hoteliers had illuminated their 'No

Vacancy' lights. After midnight, he arrived at a hotel with rooms. He checked in for two nights — the sixteenth and the seventeenth. He would leave early on the morning of the eighteenth for his trip to Lake Louise.

The room they gave him was enormous. A King-sized bed stood in an alcove near the bathroom. A low-slung dresser held a huge flatscreen television, packages of coffee and cream and sugar, and a single cup brewer. Beside it stood glass drinking glasses and ceramic mugs, not those flimsy paper or plastic things many hotels used. Next to it was a desk where the phone and a table lamp sat.

This place would suit him. Chris unpacked his shaving kit and headed for the shower. As he stood under the steaming spray, thoughts of the woman who rescued Wolfgang filled his mind. What did she look like? How would he know her? That was a straightforward decision. She'd have a Great Dane with her. How old was she? Around his age? Younger? Her profile picture gave no sign. It appeared to be knitting or crocheting, but it was hard to tell. A bigger screen would make things easier.

Twenty-Three

Lakeland College, Lloydminster, Alberta

Sept 1993

Lori stuffed her criminal background check paperwork with all her vital statistics documents in her shoulder bag. She crammed enough clothing and personal items to last a week and her books and assignments she would miss into her backpack, and left the campus for the bus stop. She had practised applying the makeup daily and now didn't resemble someone who staggered in after a night of drunken debauchery when her reflection appeared in the mirror.

She'd placed her heavier bag on the empty seat beside her when she boarded, and rested her forehead against the window. She dozed until Saskatoon when someone tapped her on the shoulder. Lori leapt out of her skin with fright.

"Sorry, didn't want to scare you. Is this seat taken?"

A thirty-ish man with wavy brown hair and a broad smile stood in the aisle. Once she regained her composure, she spoke. "No. Let me move my bag."

"I'll put it in the overhead unless there's something you

need from it?"

"No. That would be wonderful. Thanks." She needed to be left alone so she could sleep. With a seat mate, that could be impossible.

"I'm going all the way to Regina. You?"

Just what she didn't want. He would talk the entire trip. "Yes."

"I'm Dan. Dan Haines." He extended his right hand to her.

"I'm ... L ... I'm Abigail Brownell." Her heart pounded, and she willed it to slow down. She almost told a total stranger what her new identity would be. She needed to be more careful. Anyone could have a connection to her uncle and go running to him. 'Hey Gary, saw your niece. Did you know she's changing her name to Lori Brownlee?'

He swung her backpack up into the storage compartment. "What you got in this thing? Bricks?" Dan slid into the seat beside her.

About three hours later, the bus pulled into the terminal in Regina. Lori pressed her head against the seat back and stretched her neck. After a long night, she opened her eyes and blinked. By now, her seat mate had departed, and her backpack had returned to its position beside her.

Lori waited for the aisle to clear, then eased herself out of the row and hefted her bag to her shoulder. Janey stood next to the building. The girl's appearance had changed since Lori's last visit. Now, her cousin dyed her hair almost white; and beneath that jet black. And talk about skinny! Hollow cheeks, eyes sunken. The only thing that hadn't, was her penchant for baggy clothes.

For a moment, Lori lost sight of her cousin. Janey stepped forward when Lori reached the steps to alight. The girls embraced. Lori could feel every bone in her cousin's thin body. She was nothing but skin on bone, but she was strong and no doubt still had that long silky hair which covered her body.

"It's awesome to see you again, Abs," Janey said, squeezing her in a bear hug.

"And you."

Janey stepped back. "I told Mom you were coming to town for a few days. Didn't tell her for what. She said you were to stay with us, no ifs ands or buts."

That was a relief. At least Lori didn't have to pay for accommodations, but would at least help with the groceries.

They walked around the terminal, and the Chevy was in the parking lot, but not Aunt Cindy.

"Don't look so surprised. I've had my license since I turned sixteen."

"I didn't know I looked surprised." Lori had never given any thought to getting her driver's license, but she would look into lessons and such when she went back to Lloydminster. With any luck, it wouldn't cost too much.

"So when do you want to go?"

"To get my name changed?"

"No, for a tattoo. Of course, your name changed, silly," Janey said then giggled.

Lori smiled. "Not today. I need some proper sleep. Got little on the bus."

"You can crash When we get to the apartment."

At the apartment, Janey bundled Lori off to bed. The dark circles under her eyes weren't just eye makeup that had run. Rather than brew a full pot of coffee, she plugged the kettle in and settled for a cup of instant. She feared the aroma and sound of brewing coffee would prevent her cousin from getting any sleep. She curled up on the couch with her mug of Maxwell House and picked up the book she had started the previous day.

This morning, it didn't hold her interest. Was it because her cousin was here? What they would do tomorrow? Novel back on the oval coffee table, Janey picked up the *People* magazine her mother had left there. The cover article featured the battle between Charles and Diana and their fight for custody of William and Harry.

Her mother was a fan of the Royals and any time they featured a family member in a magazine, she snapped it up.

The apartment housed loads of reputable and not-so-reputable tabloids. The obsession started after her parents split up; correction, her mother threw her father out because of his predisposition for little girls — including his daughter. She discovered that when Abigail came to stay for their thirteenth birthdays; he had abused her, too.

At the time of the abuse, Janey knew hers was not a normal father-daughter relationship, but emotional blackmail and gifts kept her quiet. He always crooned how she was his special girl. She would do things mommy wouldn't. She, of those she didn't like but wanted to maintain her father's affections, surrendered to them.

Her mother worked shift work at the hospital as an X-ray technician. Her father worked straight days, so many evenings she was alone with him. That's when it happened. After her bath, Daddy came to her room. He brushed her hair. Kissed her neck. Told her she was beautiful. Sometimes his hand slid down her chest and dropped between her knees and he touched her down there. The sensation was strange, but good. She never got them right when she tried to replicate his actions. It never felt the same as when Daddy did it. Janey never told. She was a good girl — Daddy's precious girl.

She remembered the night her father left. Her mother came home early. Daddy was in her room with her. Mommy opened the door. She ran across the room, screaming at him and tearing him off her. Janey cowered in a corner. Seeing her mother in that state terrified her. Would she receive a beating, too? There were words. Angry words. Bad words. Her mother threw a lamp at him and manhandled him out of her room. Janey crept to her door and peered around the doorframe. She remembered her mother's words as she pushed him out the door. 'I don't care where you go, but don't you ever think of coming back here.'

It was after her father left Janey began starving herself. She was no longer Daddy's special girl. Her mother set her up with a child psychologist to help her see that her relationship with her father was wrong. He shouldn't have taken advantage of her like that. For a while, the sessions worked, and Janey ate. It didn't last long. She ended up in a hospital that dealt with people with eating disorders. It helped for a while. But now she was worse than before. Besides starving herself, on those occasions she ate something, she would make herself throw up afterwards — bulimia.

Janey needed to turn her life around. If she carried on this way much longer, she would kill herself. But was that what she wanted to do?

Stirring from the bedroom told her Abigail was awake.

Twenty-Four

Lori's apartment, Calgary, Alberta

May 17, 2016

It was after midnight, and Lori could not sleep. She paced around her apartment, making the loop from the living room into the foyer and back. Wolfgang followed her. Did he sense her apprehension? Dogs were intuitive, so it was possible. The Great Dane sat at her feet and rested his chin on the couch beside her.

She picked up her phone. The screen displayed several Facebook notifications, so she opened the app. Lori requested private messages when she posted about finding Wolfgang. Her post had almost one hundred comments, some of which disgusted her. In order for everyone to see her post, she had to choose the public option; otherwise, no one would.

Lori scrolled through the comments and deleted the unsavoury ones and blocked the persons responsible. At least none of them came from Gary McNeil. She had enough of him before she headed off to Lakeland College in Lloydminster. Those years in post-secondary education boosted her confidence — especially after she ditched her birth name and became Lori Brownlee. Despite losing a week of studies when she made the trip to Regina, she finished at the top of her class.

When Lori received her diplomas and achievement awards, they came framed, but she never put them on display. Why bother? No one ever came to her apartment. She had boxed them up and placed them on the floor of her bedroom closet. She displayed some certificates in her office at the bank from courses she did after she started her job there. Only clients and fellow employees saw them.

Around three in the morning, Lori fell into a restless sleep. Nightmares plagued her. Not the usual variety which related to her childhood abuse. No, these were bizarre. Some nameless, faceless entity was chasing her. She ended up in a room with mannequins rather than people dressed in mourning attire. Each one stood in a strategic location. Someone positioned a coffin against the wall. Whoever was chasing her caught her and forced her to view the corpse resting inside the box. It was her. She screamed and woke with a start. Heart pounding, sweat dripping from her forehead, Lori turned on the bedside lamp. It was her room. Her apartment. Not some freakish funeral parlour. She tried taking deep breaths to slow her heart before it exploded.

What caused that terrifying dream? Something she ate? Nervous about meeting Christopher Scott the following day? Lori grabbed her phone and searched his profile information on Facebook. He didn't post many pictures of people. Wolfgang and landscapes were the subjects of choice. The man's profile picture looked like maybe a high school photo. She remembered them. The photographer positioned you before a generic blue background. Nothing like today, where you can choose from a range of sets. One of her co-workers had photos of her children with backgrounds of bookcases, a field of flowers, and a waterfall. So different from her school days.

Lori padded to the kitchen for a glass of water. Thoughts of Christopher Scott filled her mind. What was he like? What did he look like now? How old was he? Wolfgang climbed on the bed and lay beside her when she came back to the bedroom.

"I hope I've not started any bad habits, letting you sleep with me. If I have, Chris won't be happy."

Twenty-Five

The Scott family home, Elm Street, Ottawa, Ontario

Jan 4, 2000

No thanks to Marianne's parents, Chris discovered her wake was today. His dad had found her obit in the paper that morning. He realized they blamed him for her death. He hadn't worn his suit in years, and it reeked of mothballs when he removed it from the garment bag. The smell was so strong it made his eyes water. He hung it on the back of his door while he searched his closet for a suitable shirt and tie.

Dressed in his black suit and tie, light grey shirt and shaved, Chris was ready to go. His mental state contradicted his physical one.

"Do you want me to drive you over, son?"

"No, you're okay. I was going to walk."

"Your mother and I, we'll be along sometime later."

"Thanks."

Chris's mother entered the living room from the kitchen. "Oh dear, your tie is crooked. You two …" she nodded to her husband, "neither one of you could tie a tie to save your soul."

Her fingers moved with dexterity, and she had the knot straight in no time.

"Thanks, Ma." He leaned down and kissed her on the cheek.

He didn't own a dress coat, so he shrugged on his parka as he headed out the door. The wind was brisk, and he would have frozen in just his dress clothes.

The funeral home was a fifteen-minute walk from his house, but Chris was in no rush to arrive, so he took his time. Almost half an hour had elapsed since he left the house. He climbed the steps and pushed open the door.

"What's he doing here?" Doreen Lawson said, seething with anger, when she spotted Chris in the foyer. "I don't want him anywhere near our daughter ever again."

"Doreen, he's her fiancé. He has every right to be here."

"He isn't her fiancé. He never gave her the engagement ring. Ergo, he never proposed. She was dead before that."

"Don't make a scene, Doreen. Marianne's wake isn't the time nor the place. Let's be civil and get through these next few days."

Chris entered the viewing room and strode towards them. "I'm sorry for your loss," he said as he shook William's hand.

"Thank you. Your loss, too."

"Marianne was special to many people," Chris said.

Doreen fled the room in a flood of tears. She bumped into an employee and almost knocked them to the ground. How dare he show up here? His rudeness was unforgivable. She and her husband didn't notify Chris of the arrangements on purpose. They didn't — she didn't — want him here. Why wasn't he the one shot and killed? The Scotts had five children. She only had one. Why did it have to be Marianne? She pushed open the bathroom door so hard it banged against the wall. She didn't care if she caused damage or not — she was furious.

Chris kept to the opposite side of the viewing room, but

felt Doreen's malevolent stares pierce him. He tried to ignore the woman so that he wouldn't cause a scene. Many of Marianne's co-workers passed through and expressed their condolences. Some mentioned the nasty things Mrs. Lawson had said about Chris.

A pair of friendly faces appeared not long after the afternoon viewing began. Nick and Ron entered the room, spoke with Mr. and Mrs. Lawson, then came to Chris's side.

"Holy crap, man. I still can't wrap my head around this," Nick said.

"I know," chimed in Ron. "One minute, you think you've got your whole life ahead of you, and in an instant, snuffed out."

Chris did his best to remain stoical, but his friends' comments made it difficult. "Glad you came, guys," he said as he shook their hands. Most of the time, his friends acted like clowns, but they had a serious side.

"What's with the dirty looks from Marianne's mom coming our way?" Nick asked.

Christopher faced away from the woman, and murmured, "If it were up to her, I wouldn't be here. They didn't have the decency to tell me the arrangements. I'm lucky my father found her death notice in the paper this morning."

"Unbelievable," Ron said.

"Where are your parents?" Nick asked.

"They'll be over sometime this afternoon. It's just the three of us and Marianne's parents here."

The tension in the room was palpable. Around two-thirty, Mr. and Mrs. Scott arrived and moved to where Chris stood with his friends.

"Thanks for coming." He leaned down, hugged his mother, and then shook his father's hand.

Mrs. Scott walked to the casket holding Chris's hand. "She's beautiful. I'll miss her."

"We all will, Ma."

"Melissa will come this evening. The rest of the family will be here for the funeral. You'll ride home with us when the afternoon viewing is over. A pot of stew is simmering and I'll make dumplings to have with it."

Food was not high on Chris's priorities, but his stomach growled, and his mouth watered at the mention of his mother's beef stew.

Before the afternoon ended, more people filed through. Chris breathed a sigh of relief when he stepped outside with his parents. The afternoon was more challenging than he expected.

Twenty-Six

Edmonton to Lake Louise, Alberta

May 18, 2016

Christopher got on the road early before the traffic got too heavy. Four hours, or thereabouts, separated him from Lake Louise, so he had plenty of time but was eager to reunite with his beloved Great Dane.

His hotel was close to the airport. The landing lights of the planes appeared as bright white orbs when he circled the city on the ring road as he approached on the late night/early morning of his arrival. Some took off and landed to the right side of the straight highway as he headed south. The road remained flat, but there were a few curves to ease boredom.

Fields lined both sides of the four-lane road. Farmers had worked some, but not others. Not an animal to be seen. Cash crops and hay, most likely. What appeared to be a field of winter wheat lined one side of the highway and a farm equipment dealership occupied acreage on the other.

The morning had started clear, but the farther south he drove, the cloudier the skies became. Round bales of hay sat in a field — the farm buildings in the distance. After a few hours, he passed a mileage sign; Red Deer 116 km, Calgary 203 km. The only thing keeping the boredom at bay was the advertisements on transport trailers backed up to the fences.

He needed to stop for fuel. Christopher took the exit for Lacombe and prayed they had services. How much farther was the town? A sign. One more kilometre and fingers crossed, they had fuel and coffee. He knew he was getting close when the speed limit dropped to fifty. The familiar Petro-Can signage was ahead on the right. With any luck, he could grab a hot drink, even though he preferred Tim Hortons. Chris pulled off the road and into the forecourt.

Truck fuelled and coffee in hand, Chris returned to the main road. Just before Red Deer, he turned west to avoid the traffic that had built up as commuters began their journeys to work. The road started out as four lanes, but it didn't last. It soon narrowed to a two-lane highway. If he couldn't pass, thanks to the whims of whoever drove ahead of him; he might make it to the Chateau Lake Louise before the agreed-upon time — until the unthinkable happened.

Traffic ground to a halt. No oncoming vehicles either. Accident? Most likely. He didn't need that. If the authorities didn't open the road soon, he would have to turn around and backtrack to where he left the southbound highway. Christopher pounded the steering wheel in frustration. It was his fault he was in this predicament. He left the highway one exit too soon. If he made it to the next road south, he could get on the one he wanted. Chris checked his maps app on his phone. That wouldn't work. There was no access. He'd have to continue to the roundabout or turn around and go back. He cursed himself.

During the hour he sat in traffic, he maybe moved two truck lengths. An oncoming car paused, and the driver rolled down the window. "Pull a U-turn. By the looks of things, it's going to be awhile."

"Thanks."

A siren blared in the distance, getting louder as the emergency vehicle approached. Once it passed, Chris would do as the other driver suggested. An ambulance, fire engine and police car sped by his truck. Another rescue vehicle raced past before he maneuvered his truck through a three-point turn.

Chris got his vehicle turned around and drove back to the north-south highway. This time he exited it at the proper place, but he was at least four hours away from Lake Louise and Wolfgang.

The farther out of the city he drove, the less traffic he encountered. He put his foot down and eased the truck past the hundred kilometres per hour speed limit. Chris kept the truck close to the posted speed limit and slowed when it was lower still. With any luck, he could cut some time from the journey.

The parking lots were full when Christopher arrived at his destination. He circled for an eternity before someone returned to their vehicle and left. Chris snatched the vacant spot before anyone else took it.

Twenty-Seven

Janey's childhood home, Regina, Saskatchewan

Sept 1993

Lori waited until after Aunt Cindy left for work before creeping out of the bedroom, careful not to wake her sleeping cousin. After ensuring she had all her paperwork to change her name, Lori pulled out the list she made of assignments she would miss while absent from school. She had a few hours before she had to be at the government building, so pulled out her Business Management textbook, made herself comfortable, and began reading.

Unable to settle her mind to the task at hand, Lori set the book aside. Again, she checked the documentation she brought to Regina with her to change her name. She didn't want to discover she left something behind. It was bad enough the bus between Lloydminster and Regina only ran once a week, and she would miss a week of classes.

The toilet flushed, and Janey staggered into the living room. Her legs looked like toothpicks protruding from under the thin T-shirt nightie she wore to bed. Even her shoulder blades poked against the fabric.

"Coffee?" Janey asked.

"Sure."

Her cousin padded out to the kitchen to make a pot. "Breakfast?"

"No. Too nervous to eat." Lori stood and walked to the kitchen door.

"It'll be fine. You brought all your paperwork and enough money to pay the fee. You worry too much."

Lori took the milk out of the fridge while the coffee brewed. Janey grabbed mugs. Lori fixed her coffee the minute the brewing finished and took the steaming mug to the bathroom. She'd multi-task — sort of. Coffee. Shower. More coffee. Makeup. Finish her medium roast. Brush her teeth and hair. Dress. Leave for downtown.

Things went more or less to plan, but her hand shook, applying her eyeliner, and she had to remove the makeup and start again. What would she be like later?

The girls walked from the apartment since her aunt had taken the car to work.

"Abigail Brownell?" A woman in her late thirties-early forties stood in the doorway holding a clipboard and called Lori into the office.

Janey smiled. "You're okay. I'll wait out here."

"C-can she come in with me? I'm nervous. She *is* my cousin."

"We do it one on one for confidentiality reasons."

After some deliberation, Lori said, "I'll be fine. You can wait out here, Janey."

That one word — confidentiality — made her change her mind. Uncle Gary was still in prison. Janey testified in court, too. But despite that, did she visit her father? If so, would she tell him her new identity? Thinking about the whole sordid mess gave her a headache. But it wasn't enough to make her change her mind. Before the day's end, she would no longer be Abigail Laurie Brownell but Lori Brownlee — no middle name.

The room was silent except for the tapping of the pen. Lori took a deep breath.

"Well, your paperwork is in order. Why are you petitioning for a name change?"

"My uncle sexually abused me," Lori said.

The woman nodded.

"I read you advertise the change when I did my research."

"Not always. In certain cases, we don't. If it means you're in danger of it happening again."

"I don't think so. At least not in the immediate future. I am afraid of what will happen when my uncle gets out of prison."

"We won't advertise the change then. I see you've requested our same-day service. You realize there is an extra fee for that."

"Yes."

The woman stamped the application. "You can pay the cashier at the business office. Your new ID will be ready by the close of business."

"I have to come back later?"

"We do the same day, not one hour service."

Lori left the office dejected. The last thing she wanted was to return later in the day, but she found her cousin, and they went together to pay the invoice.

"I need to come back because my stuff won't be ready until late this afternoon. We have to return before closing time."

"We can find something to kill time."

"Wascana Lake isn't far from here," Janey said. "We can walk the path along the shore as long as you don't mind geese. There are loads of them."

"I don't mind. I have to wait to get my new identity."

Janey couldn't fathom why her cousin was so hung up on this changing her name thing. Why the big deal? More hassle than it was worth in her mind. No one cared who Abigail Laurie Brownell was in the grand scheme of things. She was just another teenager from Saskatchewan. There were plenty of them — males and females.

They started out and soon were on the paved walkway along the lake.

Something ran down her upper lip from her nose. She touched the spot with the pad of her left middle finger. Blood. Her nose had bled again. Janey dug in her pockets but couldn't find anything to stop the flow. Instead, she wiped it with the sleeve of her sweatshirt.

"You okay?" Lori asked. "Your nose is bleeding."

"Yeah, happens a lot. It's nothing." She hadn't lied. It happened a lot. More than she wanted, but the psychologist had warned her when she was undergoing therapy, it could happen because of her bulimia. All the purging would cause ongoing issues with her nasal membranes, her esophagus and stomach. The woman had even tried to frighten her by mentioning esophageal cancer from the acid in her vomit. It didn't stop her from making herself throw up after eating. The only nourishment she got that stayed in her system was from the bit of milk she took in her coffee because she didn't make herself sick after drinking it.

"You're more than anorexic, aren't you?" Lori probed.

Janey nodded.

Her cousin guided her towards a bench. "I think I know the reason." She pulled up her sleeves. "I cut myself after the abuse happened and continued even after the trial. I assumed no man would want me if I made myself ugly. Is that why you're trying to kill yourself?"

"You think you're so good with your university education. You trying to analyze me? Well, don't bother," Janey spat.

Lori grabbed her cousin's arm and pushed her down. "Fine, you want to kill yourself? There are plenty of other ways. Do it and get it over."

"What?" Janey's mouth gaped open.

"Look, what your father did to us was wrong. He damaged us by his actions — our bodies and our minds. We have to be strong and rise above it."

"Spare me the lecture," Janey sniped as she wrapped her bone-thin arms around her waist.

"You know I'm right. I've been through therapy, too. I stop cutting and then something reminds me of the bad times, and I start again."

"They weren't awful. I was Daddy's special girl. He told me." A tear ran down Janey's cheek.

The abuse destroyed her cousin more than Lori imagined. But then, Uncle Gary told her similar things when he was not being mean to her. She was glad they locked him up. Exasperated, she didn't know whether to slap her cousin or hug her. Janey testifying surprised her. She heard none of what Janey said. The crown and defence lawyers didn't want any cross-contamination in their testimony. Keeping them apart was the best way to prevent that from happening. The girls saw each other afterwards when they passed in opposite directions — Janey with Aunt Cindy, her with her parents.

"I'm going back to the office. By the time I get there, the timing should be perfect. I'll see you back at the apartment?"

Janey turned her face away.

"Look, I'm sorry I was so hard on you, but someone had to say it. Am I forgiven?"

This time, her cousin rewarded her with a nod.

When Lori reached the offices, it was almost closing time. She strode to the reception desk. "I believe you have some papers for me. Abigail Laurie Brownell."

The woman at reception shuffled through the paperwork on her desk. "No."

Lori's heart sank. They promised her same-day service. "What about for a Lori Brownlee? Anything under that name?" She drummed her fingers on the counter while the woman looked.

"Nothing under that either."

She turned to leave. A somewhat overweight woman rushed into the area, waving a manila envelope. "Don't leave," she huffed, out of breath from the exertion. "Sorry, they took longer. There's nothing to worry about." The woman's face was flushed.

What did that mean?

"Here is your new identification. You are now known as Lori Brownlee." The woman handed over the package.

"Th-thank you."

Outside the building, Lori tipped her head back, squeezed her eyes shut and repeated the words thank you over and over.

Twenty-Eight

Calgary to Lake Louise, Alberta

May 18, 2016

Lori loaded Wolfgang's paraphernalia into her Mini and then returned to the apartment for the Great Dane. At least today, he didn't stink with wildfire smoke. A mobile car detailing company cleaned her vehicle, too. A fresh scent surrounded her, although in the confined space, it started out overpowering. She steered her car towards the Trans-Canada Highway and began her journey west. Google maps had told her this was the fastest route.

The day started bright and sunny. A few wisps of clouds stained the pale blue sky. The median's grass and that along the edge of the road had begun to turn green. Sprigs of grass popped up from the fields harvested the previous autumn but not yet worked.

When she reached the top of the hill, before the exit for Old Banff Coach Road, the foothills of the Rockies appeared in the distance. A herd of beef cattle grazed in a field to her left.

Clouds that started as wispy streaks became fluffy. She

couldn't differentiate between clouds or snow on the peaks.

About an hour into her journey, she was beyond the foothills and in the heart of the rugged Rocky Mountains. Lori found it difficult to concentrate; captivated by the scene unfolding around her. At the approach to Banff National Park, she almost didn't get into the through traffic lanes in time, distracted by her surroundings. The park authorities reduced the speed limit through this section of the road from one hundred and ten kilometres per hour to fifty.

Not long after the speed limit increased to ninety, a giant black bear loped across the road head of her, forcing her to jam on the brakes. Farther up the road, Lori drove through the wildlife crossing tunnel. Silly bear should have waited to cross the highway where it was safer.

The first set of traffic lights Lori encountered since leaving Calgary was at the exit of the main road and the turn towards the Chateau Lake Louise. Now she needed to concentrate, so she didn't miss her exit for the parking area. She passed a hotel on her right. Deer Lodge, so that was not the Chateau.

When she rounded the corner, the hotel she had arranged to meet Christopher near came into sight, dwarfed by the gigantic mountains. Another bend in the road and the huge parking lot came into view. It spread over both sides of the road. Once she paid for parking, she had to make her way to the spot where she told Chris she would meet him — the entrance to the underground parking.

Lori got Wolfgang out of the car after she paid for parking. She stretched, having been sitting for at least two hours behind the wheel, and checked her watch. One forty-five. They agreed to meet each other at two. Only fifteen minutes. Now to find her way to the spot. She opened the maps app on her phone. She needed to take the path at the far boundary of the parking lot and follow it until one veered off to her right. Once there, take that one, she would be right where she told Chris she'd be waiting.

With Wolfgang at her side, Lori felt safe. No one would

mess with her, only if they had a death wish. Tall, thin evergreens competed for space. Some resembled oversized toothpicks, their branches were so sparse. Scattered throughout the woods were a few white birches, leafed out in shades of pale green. If only she had more time. She would like to stay longer in this area around the Chateau. The rugged beauty of the Rockies and the tranquility of the scene made for a wonderful landscape. Not to mention the birdsong and the fresh scent of fir trees.

A whiff of cologne reached her nose. She looked over her shoulder, but nobody was there. Still, that smell was familiar. Too familiar. That was the brand Uncle Gary wore. He always smelled of it when he forced her to do things she had no desire to do. When Janey spoke of the encounters, she implied her father was always gentle with her. Never hurt her. Lori's experiences were just the opposite. He was rough, and he hurt her. One particular episode was worse than the rest. The time he shoved himself up into her bum. She cried until she had no tears left when and after he rolled off her. He called her a baby for crying. For at least a week after, she couldn't sit because the pain was so bad. She lied to her mother and said she hurt her tailbone in gym class — all the while, her uncle's eyes shooting daggers at her the entire time.

The sickening sweet scent grew more powerful, and Lori froze in her tracks. It couldn't be him. Not here. It had to be someone else who used the same product. She looked around again. Two younger guys, maybe her age, passed by her. One of them wore it. Lori heaved a sigh of relief. It wasn't her uncle, after all.

Twenty-Nine

Ottawa, Ontario

Jan 5, 2000

The entire Scott clan was present for the funeral, as his mother promised. Michael even flew back from England. Chris would have understood if his brother didn't come. It was a long way to travel to a funeral, especially for a non-family member. They held a brief visitation before the service. Several of Marianne's friends who weren't able to come the previous day were in attendance.

Mr. and Mrs. Lawson approached to say their final goodbyes first when the funeral director said it was time to close the coffin. Chris hung back. He had to say goodbye to Marianne before it was too late, but stayed back rather than encroach on their space. Mr. Lawson supported his wife as they left the room. She was in tears, but still made Chris feel uncomfortable.

Amy, Michael and Roger stood outside the chapel door. His parents were with Melissa near the foot of the casket.

Chris took a deep, ragged breath and stepped forward.

"Goodbye, Marianne. I love you," he said, then kissed her forehead. He stepped back, his eyes blurred with tears.

Melissa hugged him, and he put his arm around his youngest sibling's shoulders. Chris leaned on his parents for support as the entire family escorted him away and into their seats in the other room.

Mr. and Mrs. Scott rode in the funeral car with Chris. Marianne's parents rode in the limo behind the hearse. They were in the one after that — the other members of his family and others in their personal vehicles.

The drive to the cemetery seemed to take forever. Weather-wise, it was an appropriate day for a funeral. Gloomy, but no precipitation yet. On the outskirts of the city, the fields had a light skiff of snow on them, with the ends of cornstalks poking skyward.

Ever since Marianne's death, Chris thought about getting away from Ottawa. Load up his car and go. But where? The phrase credited to Horace Greeley, 'Go west, young man,' popped into his head. Why not? He didn't particularly like his job in Kanata, so why not quit and go west?

At the gravesite, he stood with his head bowed during the committal service. It was silent except for the occasional cough, sniffle or Mrs. Lawson. Not even birdsong. Eerie.

Chris headed straight upstairs when he arrived back home. First, he removed his suit jacket and flung the garment on the bed. The remainder of his formal attire soon followed, and he put on his comfortable jeans, T-shirt and a plaid cotton shirt.

He hauled a duffel bag out of his closet and jammed his clothes in. He would go nuts if he didn't escape from Ottawa. Last year ended in the worst possible way, and this one wasn't starting any better. There was nothing to keep him here other than a job and his parents. He had pondered the idea on the drive to the cemetery. Without Marianne, the place was empty. He'd never fill the hole left in his heart caused by her death, but Chris sure would not survive the senselessness of it all if he stuck around here.

Chris started taking armloads of his possessions downstairs and out to his car. After the third trip, his mother cornered him on his way back into the house. "What on earth are you doing?" she asked.

"Packing. Now, if you don't mind, I have more stuff to gather." He sidestepped his mother and headed back up the stairs for another load.

She stood at the foot of the staircase when he returned. "Front room. Sit. Now."

She sounded like she was telling a dog what to do.

"Christopher, what has you acting so irrational?"

"Look, Ma, I can't stay here. I need to leave. The city. The memories. They're killing me. I need to make a fresh start."

"That's just the grief talking," she said. "Give it some time. What about your job?"

"I can find another one when I get where I'm going."

"And where, pray tell, is that?"

"I'll know when I get there."

Mr. Scott entered the room, coffee mug in hand. "What's going on in here?"

"He's leaving," Mrs. Scott said.

"That true, son?"

"If Ma let me, I would be. Dad, I can't stay here. If I don't leave, I'll … I'll … I don't have a clue what I'll do. All I know is I have to escape from Ottawa."

"You made your mind up?"

"Yes."

"Well, Lucille, he is a grown man and entitled to make his own decisions. We can only hope he makes the right ones. We've brought him up well. He'll be fine."

"But that car? How far do you think it will take you?"

"All the way, I hope."

"Best of luck, son."

"Thanks, Dad."

"Bye, Ma. Love you," Chris said as he hugged his mother.

Chris picked up his last load as his family gathered in the

front hall. He said his goodbyes to them. It was hard, especially saying goodbye to Melissa. The other siblings had gone to college and university away from Ottawa. He attended the University of Ottawa, and Mel was still in elementary school. Her last year, but after the others left on their academic adventures, it was only the two of them left at home.

Standing beside his car, he took one last look at the house before easing in behind the wheel and starting the engine. After he backed out of the driveway, Chris wiped a tear from his eye and watched his family gather on the sidewalk, waving him off.

Thirty

Near the Chateau Lake Louise, Alberta

May 18, 2016

"He had to ruin everything, why?" Lori asked, choking back her anger and snatched up a stone and tossed it into the lake. "I hate that man." She grabbed another one, bigger this time, and sent it splashing into the water. "After everything he did to me, I wish he was dead."

The rock throwing continued until she tried to pick up a large one. Just her luck, it was too massive, not to mention too heavy for her to lift.

Lori collapsed on the rocky shore. Her actions caused the sleeves of her jean jacket to slide up her arms, making the ugly scars visible. She tugged them down to keep the marks hidden. Bracelets, long-sleeved tops, and sweaters year-round kept her self-inflicted disfigurement out of sight. Tears formed and pricked her eyes. She hated when she cried because of her uncle.

When was he released from prison? He got a substantial sentence. Well, at least to a fourteen-year-old girl. Why didn't they notify her?

How did he find her? Unless Wolfgang's owner was an exceptional liar, it didn't come from him. Because Lori didn't want her family to locate her and try to drag her back to Yorkton, she had changed her name. Her school chums from Lakeland College were now on social media, and some tried to hook her up with at least one site. She refused and wouldn't even let them share pictures of her lest her sleazy uncle discovered her whereabouts. It was bad enough as a child. She accepted his bribes of dolls and stuffed animals to buy her silence. The man never worked, so where did the money come from to buy these things? That came to light just after her cousin had invited her to Regina for their thirteenth birthdays. Her parents had accused her and her brother of stealing from her mother's tip jar. It had to be her uncle who took the money. Her mother's only brother.

Christopher sat back on the boulder and let Lori rant. Something occurred between her and her uncle when she was younger, and he suspected he knew what, but didn't choose to broach the subject. She would tell him if she wanted him to know. But for now, he would let her vent.

Wolfgang dropped his chin to Chris's knee, and he scratched the Great Dane's head between its ears while chewing over the previous events. Those, coupled with Lori's current state of mind, implied — no, stated — her uncle abused her as a child. Not just physical abuse, but sexual. Why else did he say those hateful words when they left him by the road to the parking lot?

He tried to push the unpleasant thoughts aside and enjoy the scenery. Tall, thin evergreens reached into the sky. The craggy peaks of the Rockies behind them wore a dusting of snow, and the the glacier-fed lake wore a gown of brilliant turquoise. Sunshine reflected like millions of diamonds on the rippling water's surface, making him squint. He unhooked his aviator sunglasses from the neck of his white T-shirt. The dazzling light on the water no longer blinded him when he wore them. The azure sky gave no hint of the devastation happening to the northeast.

Lori's sobs grew louder. Christopher walked to the water's edge and squatted beside her. He reached out and touched her on the shoulder, and she flinched. Had he frightened her? Did she think her uncle came back to attack her again? He would kick himself if his action did that to her. He didn't want to do that.

"Sorry, didn't mean to startle you," he said.

Her eyes were bloodshot and filled with tears when she looked at him. One escaped and ran down her cheek, and he brushed it away with his thumb.

Lori wanted to trust him, but her fear of men held her back. She wanted to know how her uncle found her. She had been so careful about avoiding the spotlight until now. "How? How did he find me?"

"Facebook, maybe?"

"Don't use it. Not until I found Wolfgang, and I'm not on any other social media." A little white lie. She had a locked-down Facebook account but didn't use it often.

"One of your friends or co-workers posted something with you in it?"

"No. They all know not to." Lori drew her knees up, wrapped her arms around them, and stared off into the distance.

"I didn't catch all the exchange between you and your uncle ...."

"Be glad you didn't. I still don't understand how he found me. I changed my appearance and switched from wearing glasses to contacts. Changed my hairstyle and colour. I even changed my name, and he still found me! So now I will have to do it all again." She punched her thigh.

Christopher shifted his position and sat beside her. "Wolfgang was on the news. Do you think?"

"Could be. Wait. A cameraman was filming a reporter when I went to rescue him. I couldn't bear seeing your dog looking so lost and frightened." She fiddled with the bracelets on her right wrist. "You don't suppose he filmed me? Caught me on camera, and I've been seen by all and sundry across Canada?"

Christopher took Lori's left hand to keep her from toying with her bangles. His touch was soft and not in the least bit threatening. Unlike her cold one, his was warm.

"But how did he track me here? No one knew this was my destination. Except you."

"Sorry, can't help you there."

"You told him." She yanked her hand out of his and glared at Christopher.

"I never clapped eyes on your uncle until today. I swear."

Lori lowered her gaze. She should never have turned on him. The chances of him ratting her out to her family were non-existent. At least, she thought so. Doing one good deed and saving an animal had turned into a nightmare. She was no longer safe. She needed to reinvent herself again. Leave Calgary and start over somewhere else.

Her uncle had a point. She hated to admit it. Lori Brownlee was too close to Abigail Laurie Brownell if you dropped the Abigail.

"Do you drive a Mini Cooper?" Chris asked.

"Why?"

"I glimpsed your rescuing Wolfgang. Before that, any news footage aired was just him, turning and running whenever anyone tried to approach him. Anyway, when I saw that newscast, a blue and white Mini Cooper sat on the side of the road. Maybe he saw the whole broadcast and got part of your plate number? If he has any friends on the force, who would search for the plate registered to your car ...."

"Are you a cop?" Lori asked.

"No. Have a sister who is a crime novel, television crime drama freak. She would have it all figured out if she were here."

Great. All Lori needed was some amateur sleuth involved.

Wolfgang sat facing her and put a paw on her knee. The big lummox was the best thing to come out of this mess and she would have to say goodbye to him soon. Sooner than she wanted. Why was life not simple?

He could not protect Marianne all those years ago; what made him think he could defend Lori now? His past messed him up, as hers did to her. At least they were no longer in proximity to her uncle.

"Where are you from?" he asked. "You don't have to tell me. I mean, if you're trying to fly below the radar so your people can't find you." Christopher shifted so that he faced her.

"It's kind of late for that now." Lori picked up a colourful pebble and rubbed it between her thumb and forefinger. "Saskatchewan. You?"

"Ottawa. What brought you to Alberta? Besides, you wanted to escape from home."

"I'd rather not talk about it. You?"

"Had to get out of Ontario. Too many terrible memories." He would leave it at that unless she pressed for more information, which she didn't.

"Let's go grab a coffee." Christopher stood and helped Lori to her feet. They cut through the parking lot towards the Chateau Lake Louise, with Wolfgang between them.

Buses of all shapes and sizes wound their way around the roundabout outside the hotel. People mingled outside and strolled across the road without a care, receiving blasts of a horns from angry bus drivers.

On the walk from the water, Lori looked over her shoulder. He caught her doing it but said nothing, yet her actions said it all. She was terrified her uncle still lurked in the area.

A performance car sped by them and backfired. Chris froze in his tracks. He wiped the back of his neck to remove the cold sweat that had formed below his hairline before it dripped down his back. The Rideau Centre. Marianne. Holding his hand, and then she wasn't and then she was dead.

"You okay? You look like you've seen a ghost."

"Fine. Those cars with their frigging rev limiters do my head in every time I hear them."

"I know what you mean. They sound kind of like a gun."

They approached a coffee shop with outdoor tables. Christopher steered Lori to a vacant one. "You and Wolfie save this table, and I'll go get us a drink. What do you take in yours?"

"Cream and sugar. Two of each."

"Ah, a double-double."

"My mother works — worked at Tim Hortons. You would have known if I had said that." She dropped her gaze to her lap.

Chris smiled and walked to the coffee bar. The lineup for service was long, but the staff was efficient, and soon he had their double-doubles and was back outside where he had left her minding his dog.

"I don't think you have to worry about your uncle here. Too many people around."

"I hope you're right." Lori removed the top from her coffee and took a sip. "It was a shock hearing his voice, not to mention smelling his cologne. He's been in jail since I was fourteen. I thought he was still in there." She fidgeted with the lid.

The encounter with her uncle scared Lori. Chris had to tread with care lest he spooked her more than she already was.

Thirty-One

Near the Chateau Lake Louise, Alberta

May 18, 2016

Lori relaxed in Christopher's company. He seemed to be a proper gentleman, much like her father. She missed her dad and almost contacted him, but fear of her uncle discovering her whereabouts held her back. Still, she couldn't discuss the abuse meted out by Uncle Gary with her dad. When she worked up the nerve to tell her mother about it, she didn't believe Lori. Not until Aunt Cindy drove her home and everything blew up that her mother realized she had been wrong.

She took in the scenery now that she was less frightened. A few fluffy clouds dotted the blue sky. Down the street to her right, a horse-drawn wagon stood next to the sidewalk. From her vantage point, no passengers were onboard; the lone occupant — the driver.

"Here you go. One large double-double." He sat a paper cup wearing a protective sleeve on the table in front of her.

"Thanks."

Should the questions arise, how much of her past did she want to share? So far, she told him she came from Saskatchewan and nothing else. Chris had something in his past, too. Terrible memories in Ontario. Did she dare ask him to elaborate?

Lori stole the occasional glance at Chris as he sipped his coffee, his gaze elsewhere. She dipped her head when he turned back towards her, not wanting him to know she'd been staring at him. Still, his mahogany brown eyes bored into her, as if trying to read her innermost thoughts.

The garment slipped off her left shoulder when she tugged down her jean jacket sleeves again to hide her scars. That, in turn, dragged the long-sleeved T-shirt she wore underneath, exposing the tattoo which started on her collarbone and continued down her arm. She adjusted the coat and covered the markings. A quick look at her companion said he didn't see it. His contemplative expression was once again on someone or something else. Or he was too much of a gentleman to say anything.

She got the tattoo and sleeve done over the course of a few sessions. Every one hurt as much as the previous. It was one of those things she tried to make herself appear unattractive to men. At least the right men. After all, girls with tattoos were rough and, in some communities, tarts. Not the type the church-going mothers wanted their sons dating.

"What made you choose this location to return Wolfgang?"

"I haven't been here, but everything says it's beautiful. Pictures of the place are gorgeous, and best of all, there are always hordes of people around. And the photos didn't lie. This place is breathtaking."

He had to agree with her. Day-trippers packed the parking lot. And over here? Buses. Mini-buses and full-sized coaches traversed the roundabout outside the hotel.

"Any other reason?"

"I preferred not to meet a stranger at my place."

"Got it. I could be an axe murderer, serial killer or something." Chris said as he chuckled and received an icy stare for his troubles. "Sorry for my sick sense of humour."

"You're forgiven." Lori sipped her coffee.

He tried hard not to gawp, but it was difficult. Her self-mutilation drew his eyes to Lori's wrists. On a warm day like today, she had to be roasting in that jean jacket. He found it hot in just his shirt sleeves. Earlier, he glimpsed her scars, but didn't know how many and how bad they were. He also noticed some tattoos on her shoulder before Lori covered herself. At least, that's what he thought the design was. He couldn't tell if it was a tattoo or the pattern on the shirt she wore under her jacket.

Chris had read of people's self-harming by cutting and burning themselves. One of Marianne's classmates from Lisgar Collegiate had done it to herself. The underside of the girl's arms was a solid mass of scar tissue from her wrists to her armpits. That was all he could recall of the girl.

How far up her arms did Lori's scars go? How severe were they? The brief time her raised sleeves exposed her wrists didn't give him enough to get a good idea. Better yet, why did he care? He came to collect his dog, not begin a meaningful relationship with a young woman.

Chris had his dog, so could get up and leave, but something compelled him to stay. That jerk who upset her might still lurk in the area waiting for her to be on her own. Was that it? Was he worried about that and didn't want to leave Lori alone?

If it weren't for Marianne's death, Chris wouldn't have moved to Fort McMurray and gotten a job with SUNCOR. Wolfgang wouldn't have run off, if not for the wildfire and the evacuation. Lori wouldn't have rescued him, and he wouldn't be sitting across the table from her now. There were too many ifs.

Lori fidgeted with the sleeve surrounding her paper cup. She drank most of the coffee, but now it was cold.

"Are you staying here at the hotel?" Chris asked.

"I came this morning. I planned to go home once I returned your dog." So why did she tell him anything? She had no reason to divulge that much information. Was he looking for something she wasn't prepared to give him? "What about you?"

"I hadn't thought that far ahead. I can't go back to Fort Mac yet. Not until the ..." his voice trailed off.

Lori knew she couldn't afford to stay in a place like the Chateau Lake Louise. It was beyond her budget. She only lived a few hours away, so she could make it a day trip.

"What's the latest news about the fire?" she asked.

"Still raging and consuming everything in its path."

"Sorry. Do you think you'll stay here until you can go back home?" Within a few hours of meeting him, she went again, getting too involved with him.

"I don't think the insurance company will spring for something this lavish. If I have fire coverage."

"You mean you might not be?" She leaned forward.

"Not all policies cover wildfires. I need to contact my company and find out if I'm one of the lucky ones who do."

"Why don't we walk around?" Lori suggested as she stood. Sitting in one place in the open with her uncle around made her uncomfortable. But, at least if she kept moving, she might evade him.

Christopher took her cup and dropped it and his own in the nearby trash can.

Whatever side he intended on having Wolfgang on was the side Lori was choosing. At least there would be a dog between them.

Chris held Wolfgang's leash in his right hand. Lori walked on the other side of the dog. He would rather she walked closer to him, but if having the Great Dane between them made her feel secure, then so be it.

The couple walked along one of the hiking trails that meandered around the lake. They turned and walked back in the opposite direction, when the Lake Agnes Trail and the Lake Louise Lakeshore Trail intersected.

Chris stole glances at Lori. She continued to look over her

shoulder, but not as often. Was she becoming more comfortable in his company? Less worried that her uncle was still in the area? The man would be far away from here if he had half a brain.

Why was he obsessed with this woman? Was it because of her vulnerability? Someone she should have been able to trust hurt her? He needed to go back to his truck, load Wolfgang inside, drive to a pet-friendly hotel, and stay there for the all-clear to return to Fort Mac. That begged the question: what waited for him when he returned?

Thirty -Two

Lori's apartment, Calgary, Alberta

May 19, 2016

Lori woke with a start. The alarm didn't go off and frighten her. She didn't set it at night because she hadn't returned to work. Was it some other noise? Was someone trying to break into her apartment? She couldn't see the door from her bedroom.

Her navy housecoat lay on the bottom of the bed. She grabbed the velour bathrobe and put it on as she walked towards the apartment's entrance. The peephole limited the view, but the hallway appeared empty. She took the chain off the latch and opened her door a crack — no one or nothing out there.

Her imagination had to be playing tricks on her. Did the scratching sound come from the flat across the hall? Lori crept back inside, ensured she locked the door, and stopped in the bathroom.

She lived in a secure building, so why the sudden paranoia? Noises never bothered her in all the years she lived alone. But, then her uncle wasn't on the prowl. Did he follow her when she left Lake Louise? What kind of vehicle did he drive? She encountered him on foot; his usual cocky swagger. Had he followed her Mini, and she wouldn't know. The vehicle behind her was Christopher's red Ram truck.

He didn't follow her to her place, but back to Calgary. The heavy traffic meant she got through some traffic lights Chris didn't, and she lost him before she arrived home. Did Uncle Gary follow Chris? Now she was being ridiculous. Coffee. She needed the caffeine jolt. Maybe after that, she'd start thinking more rationally.

Lori inserted a light roast pod in her coffeemaker, filled the water reservoir, and started the brew cycle. No cup. She snatched one from the drainboard and shoved it in place before any of her morning beverage spewed out and all over the counter.

Her apartment was safe if she kept her door locked and the chain on. She needed to get a grip. No one could gain access. They had to be buzzed in by another tenant or wedge their foot in the security door.

Thirty-Three

Calgary, Alberta

May 20, 2016

The Travelodge was an okay place to stay, but not home. Clean and pet-friendly made his time bearable. Besides, until the authorities gave the all-clear and everyone could return to Fort Mac, he couldn't go anywhere. At least it put him close to Lori's apartment, so they were able to spend some time together. An off-leash dog park was close to her place, according to her, and they planned to take Wolfgang today.

After he ate breakfast and fed Wolfgang, he bundled the dog into the truck and headed across town to her apartment. There was a small park on Lori's street, but the Great Dane couldn't run free so it was off the board.

Chris enjoyed his time in her company. Despite the events of her past, she could be a fun-loving girl. They'd only known each other a few weeks if you counted her posting on Facebook that she rescued his dog. They only knew one another face-to-face for two days.

Sometimes, he felt as if he were cheating on Marianne

while he was in Lori's company. He had been unable to form a relationship with a woman since her death. He had felt unfaithful to his former girlfriend on other occasions. About half a dozen young women worked at SUNCOR, but if he dated any of them, it was only the once. They weren't even proper one-night stands because there was no sex involved, which suited Christopher just fine.

Lori was different. She could be a prospect once he got better acquainted with her. He admired her spunk, even when she ranted over her uncle's unexpected and unwanted appearance. She was vulnerable, but also a formidable adversary. Because of her childhood, being in a relationship might not be probable. The way she recoiled when he put his arm around her shoulders said no. She'd warmed since then, and if he touched her, accidentally or otherwise, she didn't shy away from him.

When Lori let him into her apartment, she wore cut-off jean shorts, high-top running shoes, and a hoodie. It was not cold in her apartment, nor was it that cold outside. He'd glimpsed her scars that first day when she threw stones into the lake. With any luck, she would open up to him at the dog park.

"Want a coffee? I'm a bit late getting around this morning. I didn't sleep well last night."

"Sure."

He sat at the small drop-leaf table pushed against the wall opposite the sink.

"Breakfast blend or Colombian?" Lori asked as she got the cream out of the fridge and set it beside the sugar.

"Whatever's easiest."

"Both the same."

The toaster popped, ending their conversation.

"You eat yet? All I can offer is toast and maybe some jam or peanut butter."

"I grabbed a bite at the hotel before I came over."

Lori placed a steaming mug of coffee on the table. "Here you go."

She started another brew in the coffeemaker.

"Yeah, so the dog park isn't far away. About ten minutes." Lori sat down across from Christopher and prepared her coffee. "There are a couple farther west if that one is too busy."

"If it's too busy, I'll keep Wolfie on his leash. Don't forget your toast."

She put the single slice on a plate and grabbed a knife from the drawer. The small jar of peanut butter sat on the table, and she slathered on a thick layer. "You sure you don't want any?"

"I'm good. You eat."

After eating, she put the dishes in the sink and finished her coffee.

"Okay, let's go." Lori paused at the console table in the hall and picked up her phone and keys.

The park was quiet for a Friday. "Most of the time, this place is crowded," she observed.

Chris unhooked the leash and tossed a stick for Wolfgang to chase. He took Lori's hand as they strolled through the green space. She appreciated his warm hand because her hands were always cold.

"There aren't any benches, so if you want to, we'll have to sit on the ground."

"We'll keep walking for now."

"Tell me about your house in Fort Mac," she said as she placed her right hand on his upper arm.

"Huge. Too big for just one person. I keep the upstairs closed off. Everything I need is on the main level, the basement or garage."

"Sounds lonely. You rattling around on your own." Her apartment could be lonely and it was a fraction of the size of the house Chris described.

"Yeah, until Wolfgang came along. He doesn't say much, but that's okay. When I'm home, I'm catching up on what I let go while away on the job. Mowing the lawn in the summer. Clearing snow in the winter."

"You don't commute every day?"

"No. I live in the work camp for two weeks; then I'm home for two."

"I didn't know. None of my clients work in that industry."

"That's okay. I would have met you sooner but we couldn't leave the camp. The sky was black; and ash rained down on us, yet they told us to keep working."

"It must have been terrifying. I only got a brief taste when I rescued Wolfgang. It scared me to death."

"Let's go sit on that tree stump," Chris said.

They sat down, and Chris took both her hands in his. "You have been through scarier things in your life than fire."

"Wh-why do you say that?" She yanked her hands away.

"I saw your wrists the other day. Heard the hateful things your uncle spewed about you."

Lori's face lost all colour. She looked like she might faint. Chris bundled her into his arms and held her close. She didn't pull back like she did the first time he tried to place his arm around her. And that was a protective gesture.

"You don't have to, but you may feel better if you tell me."

"Thanks to my uncle, I'm no longer whole. Is that what you mean?"

"Whole enough for me." Where did that come from? Was he ready to commit? Things were moving too fast for his liking. He still had to reconcile his feelings of cheating on his deceased girlfriend.

Lori wriggled out of his arms, tears streaming down her face.

"Hey, hey, don't cry." Chris wiped her tears with his thumbs. "At this stage of our lives, I wouldn't have expected you to be a virgin. I just don't like the way you lost your virginity." Again, he gathered her into his arms and close to him. Her arms encircled his waist.

After a few moments in Christopher's embrace, Lori leapt to her feet. She couldn't do this. How could she? Men terrified her. Her uncle had seen to that. Not once, when he had taken advantage of her, did Lori like it. She hated it. Hated him — hated the pain he caused during their encounters.

Chris crossed the line — a line she didn't want anyone to cross. Ever!

In an instant, he stood next to her. "I'm sorry. I didn't mean to upset you. The things your uncle said the other day and your reaction to seeing him; I knew something funky happened between you." His arms encircled her, and he pulled her close to him. "He won't touch you again."

"How do you know?" she snuffled.

"He needs to go through me first."

A protector. A knight in shining armour. Where was he when she needed him as a child and into her teens? Chris was right that her uncle wouldn't touch her again. She was too old now. He preferred children. Is that why Ricky always went to Grandpa Brownell's farm every summer? Did Gary try it on with him, too? She was only aware of Janey. That came out during her trip to her cousin's home in Regina to commemorate their thirteenth birthdays. How many others did her uncle molest?

A cold nose touched her bare leg, and she flinched.

"Oh, I've just snotted all over your shirt."

Christopher chuckled. "Is that all you're worried about? A little mucus?"

She stammered and tried to wipe it away, but he took her wrist, parted the bracelets and planted a soft kiss on the scars beneath. He brushed her tears away with his thumbs, then pulled her close to him again.

"You're a beautiful woman, Lori. You deserve a man who will treat you with respect. Not take advantage of you whenever he wants. With the right person, making love is beautiful, not anything close to what your uncle did to you."

"And you know this how?"

"Trust me." He bent down and kissed her forehead.

Chris tried to reconcile his feelings for the girl in his arms. It couldn't be love. At least not this soon. It was only a few days. Was it because he wasn't able to protect Marianne, and she died? Was he projecting his feelings for his dead not-quite fiancée towards Lori? What a mess. What a huge mess. One of these days, he would tell her about what happened all those years ago, but not today. For now, he just wanted to enjoy her company.

Thirty-Four

Lori's apartment, Calgary, Alberta

June 1, 2016

Lori placed a pod of breakfast blend in her coffee maker, started the machine running, and turned on the news. The authorities deemed the city of Fort Mac safe, and people could come back home. Rather than have a massive influx of people, only specific neighbourhoods would return at a time. She wouldn't have much time with Christopher and Wolfgang.

The time had flown by since she met him at Lake Louise to return the dog. She was unsure if a physical relationship with Chris was possible. They'd cuddled, held hands, and kissed. He had held her when she had a meltdown. But could she make love with him? Her uncle had ruined her on that score.

She powered up her laptop and checked her emails while she sipped her light roast. One was from her boss, asking when she would return to work. She sent back a quick response of 'don't know. Will keep you posted.' The rest of her inbox was newsletters she subscribed to or junk mail and phishing scams.

Something on the street caught her attention when she

stood to take her empty mug to the kitchen. A closer inspection revealed her uncle standing on the far sidewalk, looking at her building. Her hand trembled, and the cup slipped out of her fingers and crashed on the floor. The rest of the mug shattered after the handle broke.

In her haste to put the chain on, Lori stepped on a piece of broken glass and cut her foot. She hopped from that point to the door and secured the lock; cursing her stupidity for not paying attention to where she placed her feet, she hobbled to the bathroom. Lori hauled a gauze pad, first aid tape, peroxide and antibiotic cream out of the medicine cabinet over the sink. She sat on the toilet lid and lifted her foot to inspect the damage. She pulled on the shard, but it hurt too much.

Lori's cell phone was in her bedroom, so she worked her way down the hallway, avoiding the living room where the accident occurred. For the most part, she texted or used Messenger to contact Chris. However, today was far from ordinary. Hysteria was setting in. She looked up Christopher in her contacts and then pressed the green telephone receiver icon. Pick up, pick up, pick up, she urged. He answered as she was about to disconnect the call.

"Hi."

"It's awful. He's here. He found me," Lori got out between sobs.

"What? Who found you? Slow down."

"My uncle — Gary. He's on the street across from the apartment. I-I stepped on broken glass when I put the chain on the door. The piece is still in my foot." She paused and took a breath.

"Okay. Stay right where you are. I'll be there as quick as I can."

"Th-thank you."

Lori disconnected the call. She hoped it wouldn't take long for Chris to reach her. She stretched to snatch a look out the window. Her uncle was still on the sidewalk, but now he was with someone else. One of her neighbours, she guessed.

"Come on, Wolfie. Lori needs us."

The Great Dane put his head back on the bed she bought for him.

Chris picked up the leash and shook the lead. The clip rattled, and the dog leapt to its feet. With the lead fastened, they headed towards the truck. Things would have been easier if the room had an outside entrance. He parked his truck outside the window to monitor it. Instead, they walked down the corridor, exited through the lobby, and around the corner of the building. The extra steps wasted valuable time.

No one was on the street when Chris pulled around the corner. Had she jumped to conclusions? Had the man forced his way into her apartment? He parked on the street, blocking Lori's Mini.

Thankful that she gave him a key to the security door; he gained access to the private area of the building without having to bother someone else to buzz him through. Once inside, he raised his hand to knock on the door, but it was ajar. Could that woman not listen for once? He'd told her to keep the door closed and the chain on until he got there. Did she? No. And worse, she'd opened her apartment to someone. Chris gave the heavy door a push, then stepped into the hall.

The living room was empty, but a news channel blared. Blood and broken ceramic littered the floor. "Lori?" He called.

"I-in here."

The voice came from the bathroom.

"Are you okay?"

"No."

Chris tried the knob, and the door opened. Lori sat on the floor in the corner by the sink. "I told you not to open the door until I arrived." He squatted beside her and rubbed his neck.

"I didn't. I saw you pull up out front."

"You know what I meant."

"Was he still out there?"

"No. Not a soul on the street. Maybe it wasn't him. Maybe it was the way the light hit the guy."

"I know what my uncle looks like." Her voice dripped with sarcasm.

"Let's forget about that and get your foot fixed up, eh?"

Lori swivelled on the floor and put her injured foot on Chris's thigh.

He gripped her ankle against his leg. "That's not so bad."

"Easy for you to say. It isn't in the bottom of your foot."

"All right. I'm going to yank that sucker out of there, okay?"

She nodded.

"One … two … three." Christopher plucked the piece of the broken coffee mug out of the sole of her foot.

The first aid supplies lay on the counter, so he cleaned her injury and dressed it. "Think you can stand on it?"

Lori scrambled to her feet and put pressure on the injured one.

"You're not leaving this room without shoes. I'll be right back."

Christopher took her running shoes to the bathroom. "Here you go. I'll clean up the mess while you get them on your feet."

He took the small wastebasket from the bathroom with him, picked up the big chunks of the coffee mug, and tossed them in. No smaller pieces were visible, but he pulled the vacuum cleaner out of the closet and went over the floor. A few tiny shards rattled against the machine's canister when they were sucked up.

The entire time, Wolfgang remained by the door as if guarding the apartment.

"Okay, Wolfie, you can come in now. Nothing to hurt your feet in here." The dog flopped next to the couch.

Blood droplets remained on the floor, but Chris had done more than his fair share with doctoring Lori's foot and picking up the broken mug. She could mop her floors.

His thoughts turned back to the eve of the millennium when Marianne died. Except then, it was not just drops that put a spreading pool of blood beneath her and the growing stain on her stomach. He was not afraid of blood, but seeing it brought back those awful memories.

Thirty-Five

Lori's apartment, Calgary, Alberta

June 1, 2016

Lori tested her foot again with her shoes on. The support in her shoes irritated the tender arch of her foot, but not to the point she couldn't put pressure on it.

She found Chris and Wolfgang in the living room.

"He knows where I live. What am I going to do?" she cried.

Chris patted the couch beside him. "For a start, you're going to sit here and calm down."

His arm encircled her shoulder when she sat, and he held her close to him. His body radiated heat, and the spicy scent of his body wash wafted towards her nose. Safety and security enveloped her like a warm blanket.

"Why don't you go back to Saskatchewan and see your parents?"

"Yorkton is the last place I want to be, seeing how that man is out of prison."

"It might help you."

Lori raised her head and stared at him. She just told him the name of her hometown. Without thinking, she told him where she hailed from, and that was the last thing Lori wanted. Her origins must remain secret. At least she didn't spew her complete address.

"He found you in Lake Louise, and now you say you've seen him outside your apartment. You're safer there than here if he's planning some kind of payback."

"You think he's come after me? He's going to hurt me, or worse?" Lori jumped off the couch.

Christopher had put his size twelves in but good. Not just one, but both. Talk about dumb moves. He stood and moved to her side to comfort her. "Come on. No one will hurt you as long as I'm here."

"B-but you won't always be here."

She was right. Once the authorities gave Chris's neighbourhood the green light to return, he and Wolfgang would go back to Beacon Hill. Lori would be alone here in Calgary. "You could always come with me."

The words spilled out before he thought about what he said. It was too soon, wasn't it? Not too soon after Marianne's death — seventeen years ago — but too soon for him and Lori. Chris, now over forty, hadn't been in a lasting relationship with a woman since Marianne. Her death messed him up big time. He would have to tell Lori about his past. He had figured hers out, and she confirmed his thinking. But, so far, no response to his suggestion.

"You want me? Me with all my baggage and warts?"

He didn't reply to her questions. "You need to sit down. I have something to tell you." He led her back to the sofa, sat her down then joined her. Chris rooted in his front pocket for his wallet.

Oh, God. The man had a wife or a girlfriend. He … Lori couldn't accept Chris belonged to someone else. She kept her eyes down, sneaking peeks at Chris's actions. He had taken his wallet out and now held something in his hand.

"This is Marianne. Marianne Lawson."

A girlfriend. Her first normal relationship, albeit in the early stages, with a guy, and she's just his bit on the side. Not that they were in a proper relationship. They were just friends.

"Marianne is dead. I've carried her grade eleven high school photo since we started dating that year."

Was he trying to con her with the dead wife, dead girlfriend line? She wouldn't fall for that. After all, she was not born yesterday, nor did she fall off a turnip truck. Lori looked at him, and his eyes were red and glassy. Either this guy was an excellent actor, or he was not lying to her. She preferred to think the latter and took the photo from him. The girl in the picture looked perfect. Too perfect. Barbie and Ken perfect. Wavy auburn hair, sparkling green eyes, and a dazzling smile. She handed the photograph back. At least the girl was dead because Lori couldn't compete with all that perfection.

"It's been almost sixteen and a half years since her death."

Did Lori want to know? Of course. Did she die from cancer or some other disease? A car accident? "How?"

"She died on Dec 31st, 1999. The world would end at midnight. Mine ended around five o'clock that night."

She remembered all the hype. Computers would crash. The Y2K bug. She didn't care when this woman died. She wanted to know *how*. Chris was having a hard time telling her.

"She worked as a nurse, and I picked her up after her shift. Our shifts didn't align so the last time we saw each other was Christmas Day. I'd bought her an engagement ring and we were on the way to pick it up. I planned to propose to her in the jewellery store."

"But ..." There was always a but. Lori fidgeted with her bracelets.

"We never got that far. We'd gotten off the elevator and into the main corridor on the same level as the shop when the shooter fired and hit her. She died there in my arms. I couldn't save her. Couldn't protect her. I tried, but I failed." Chris drew a ragged breath.

Lori had her arms around him and held his head against her chest. What he went through was awful, even worse than her childhood trauma. She knew what he meant when Chris told her about the right relationship. He had it with Marianne.

An enormous weight rose from Christopher's shoulders. He had told no one what had happened that night. His friends and family were all Ottawa natives. He didn't need to — they knew. The television news and the newspapers covered the tragic event. They heard more on the radio. The emotional toll the tragedy took on him was what they didn't realize. The media couldn't capture that. Reporters harassed his family to get interviews with their bereft son and them. He assumed they harangued Mr. And Mrs. Lawson, too.

He asked Lori to go back to Fort Mac with him. Did he mean it? Or was it a suggestion so that he wouldn't have to be alone? Marianne would always be a part of him, but could he let her go?

And Lori. Damaged goods thanks to her uncle. She'd self-harmed for years. A family member she should have been able to trust, took advantage of her. Could she be everything he needed? He had been gentle, not quite the right word, but it worked, from when he put two and two together and came up with the correct answer. Patient was a better one.

In the short time he'd known her; a few occasions arose where he wanted to pull her into his arms and kiss her. Instead, he had settled for hugs, holding hands, a kiss on the cheek, a peck on the lips, and sitting snuggled side by side. He didn't need to send her into a meltdown by doing something her uncle had done. It would be difficult, but it would be worth it.

"You asked me something earlier, and I didn't answer it. Do you want to ask me again?" Chris asked.

"What was that?"

"Something to do with baggage."

"Oh yeah. I remember what it was," Lori said. "You want me? Me with all my baggage and warts?"

"Yes, I do, Lori Brownlee. I do."

His eyes locked on hers. The darkness from the past which filled Lori's eyes faded. As it did, the sparkling emerald green took over. Christopher pulled her to him and touched his lips to hers. This time it was a full-blown lingering kiss. Best of all, she didn't freak out.

Thirty-Six

Lori's apartment, Calgary, Alberta

June 2, 2016

The glowing red numerals on the alarm clock read five forty-five. Lori would catch her mother before she left for work if she still worked at her server's job at Tim Hortons if she made the call now. Lori held her cell phone with her finger poised to hit the call button, but hesitated. Could she make the first move? Should she? Did her mother know Gary was out of prison? After a long pause, she pushed the button. She was about to disconnect when her mother picked up.

"Hello."

"Hi, Mom, it's me, Lor … Abigail." It seemed strange to use her given name. She hadn't been that girl in twenty years.

"Abigail. It's so good to hear your voice. I saw you on TV when you rescued that horse of a dog."

The tone of the conversation then changed.

"You realize I've been going out of my mind with worry, thinking someone hurt you or killed you?"

"I'm sorry, Mom, but I had to disappear. I figured Uncle

Gary would come after me when he got out. Bad enough he found me in Lake Louise a couple of weeks ago, but I saw him outside my apartment the other day."

"Why would my brother look for you?"

"Get me back for getting him arrested, testifying in court." Until Christopher mentioned the possibility, revenge for incarceration never entered her mind. She always thought he wanted more of the same, which landed him in jail to begin with.

"You weren't the only one who testified. Janey did, too."

Her mother was not making this easy for her. Did the woman still believe her brother to be innocent? Was the woman delusional? Gary McNeil was far from innocent. "I know, Mother." During the trial, neither girl sat in the main courtroom. They were in rooms next door in front of cameras. Their testimony to the judge and the others in the public gallery broadcast via closed circuit television.

"I met a man. He's kind, and he's good to me. He works in the oil sands, and the Great Dane I rescued is his."

"That's nice."

Her mother's tone was far from sincere.

Lori changed the subject. "How are Dad and Ricky?"

A huff sounded across the line.

"What?"

"Your father hasn't been right since you disappeared. He had a heart attack and ended up having open heart surgery. You'd know if you didn't pull that stunt. Your grandfather passed away two years ago, and Ricky inherited the farm. At least it stayed in the family."

Another dig. How could the woman be so cruel? Lori wanted to mend fences. Try to get back to where they were before her uncle moved into their lives.

"Dad on the road now?"

"Yes."

"When is he due home?"

"He should be back the day after tomorrow."

"Tell Dad I love him, and I'll call again when he's home so I can speak to him. Bye, Mom." Lori pressed the disconnect button. She wanted to tell her mother more about Christopher. She was glad it was only a phone call, not an in-person visit. That would have been too much.

Grandpa Brownell dead. He was always an old man to her. White-haired and moustache that matched, he was tall and thin and wore a weathered Fedora and long-sleeved white cotton shirts, even in the heat of summer. Grandma Brownell died when Lori was a little girl. She didn't remember her face but recalled the woman's stature — stout with an ample bosom and hugs at the ready any time you needed or wanted one. The woman baked huge molasses cookies. The farmhouse's kitchen was always filled with the mouth-watering aroma when they visited on Sundays. She salivated just thinking about them.

Her brother always liked the farm and the animals. Lori, not so much.

She needed to talk to her brother. With any luck, he would be more amiable than her mother. Somewhere, she had the phone number for the farm squirrelled away. But where and could she find it? Handwritten and not stored it in her phone or other electronic device. Where did she stash that old address book? She didn't take many things from the house in Yorkton when she attended Lakeland College, but she definitely took it.

A search of the hall closet revealed nothing other than coats, boots, shoes, a vacuum cleaner, a mop and a bucket. Shoes, slippers, purses and the box containing her framed diplomas and awards littered the floor of her bedroom closet. Was it on the shelf above the chaos?

Lori carried a chair in from the kitchen to stand on. Way back in the corner sat a box the size that held a pair of winter boots at one time. She stretched but could not reach it. Her fingers brushed the side. With the chair moved closer, she succeeded. Dust covered the top of the box. What treasures were inside? Lori blew on it. Dust went up her nose, and she sneezed.

With caution, she climbed down from the chair, took the box with its bounty to the kitchen table, and removed the lid.

Her Saskatchewan Roughriders pennant lay on top. It seemed like a lifetime ago she went to the game with her aunt and cousin. Beneath it was a legal-sized manila envelope. Lori removed the papers. They were the legal documents from when she changed her name. Another envelope contained some old family photos. Ricky and her as kids sporting gap-toothed smiles. That one was before Uncle Gary had moved in and ruined her life.

Lori pulled out two of her high school photos from grades ten and twelve. At least, that was what her loopy script on the backs read. None for the odd-numbered years. Strange. She had a haunted look in both photos — short hair. The exact opposite of the gorgeous girl Christopher planned to marry before a cruel twist of fate struck, ending those plans once and for all.

A piece of jewellery would fit in a small velvet-covered box. She lifted the hinged top. Inside, protected in plastic, was the Stirling silver locket that once belonged to her great-grandmother. She took the piece out and opened it, but there was no picture inside. This was one of Lori's favourite things when she was little, and although she didn't wear it often, she cherished it.

At last, Lori found the address book, which was the initial purpose of her quest, although she enjoyed her trip down memory lane. She flipped through the pages until she found the one she wanted.

She wouldn't call her brother now. This time of year, they'd be cutting hay. She wouldn't be able to contact Ricky until after sundown. Even if he came in for supper, he would return to the barn or the fields afterwards. She remembered that from her weekly visits as a child.

Was her brother married? Did he have children? She didn't ask her mother. She'd never even thought of that. But she hoped Gary wasn't nearby if he was and did.

Christopher disconnected the call. He had been dealing with his insurance company since they evacuated the Millennium Lodge. He listened to recording after recording before he reached a human at the branch. Had he been able to deal with his broker in Fort Mac, it would have been much better.

He received some decent news and couldn't wait to share his good fortune with Lori. Chris punched her number into his cell phone. "Hey," he said when she picked up. "I got some fantastic news just now."

"Why don't you come for supper? Say five-ish? You can tell me then."

"I guess I can wait that long."

"I have some news to share with you, too. Make sure you bring Wolfgang."

Chris pictured her wearing that mischievous grin that didn't appear often enough. Her eyes sparkled when she smiled.

"Okay."

"If you don't bring Wolfie, I'm cancelling the invitation."

"Wolfgang and I will be there about five o'clock," Chris said and ended the call.

She was up to something. Chris knew it. But what? He would find out soon enough. It was just after three. He had plenty of time before he had to be at Lori's apartment. Time to take the Great Dane for a walk, then come back and shower and head over. The traffic could be murder at that time of day, so he'd leave a bit earlier and give himself plenty of time.

Lori left the address book out of the box, opened to the page with the phone number. With Christopher coming over for supper, she needed to make a start on it. Not anything fancy: spaghetti, Caesar salad and garlic bread. Because she lived alone, she rarely cooked fancy meals. Even the pasta sauce for tonight came out of a can, but she would add some extra seasoning, ground meat, chopped onion, mushrooms and garlic, and dress it up a bit more.

She bumped the box against a large plastic bag when she put it back on the shelf. Balls of yarn tumbled out, along with some half-finished projects, the knitting needles, or crochet hooks still attached. Since the Fort Mac fire her interest in her hobby had waned, too preoccupied with the disaster. And now, with her uncle finding her and stalking her, she didn't have time. Although she thought of a few painful things to do to him with one of those pointy weapons. Sterilization by knitting needle. Blindness by knitting needle. Lobotomy by knitting needle.

Even though she enjoyed those thoughts, she was done. Lori shoved the craft supplies back into the bag, but rather than return the filled bag to the shelf, she stuffed it on the floor with her other detritus. The next time she opened the closet door, she didn't need to be bombed.

Right. Spaghetti sauce. Lori rooted through the cupboards, searching for the can. Upper cabinets, lower ones. Nothing. She needed to make a trip to the grocery store. She had plenty of time. Since she had to go for that, she grabbed a pen and a piece of scrap paper and wrote a list.

She could walk to the supermarket, but with the number of things on her list, she couldn't carry them all back if she was on foot. Lori grabbed her reusable bags from the hall closet, took her keys off the hook, and headed out the door. She wanted everything tonight to be just right.

Chris was coming to eat for the first time. They had spent plenty of time together, but it was before meals or after and if they ate together, it was in a restaurant.

By four-thirty, the sauce simmered on the stove. She put the salad in the fridge. Lori would pour the dressing on the greens just before she served them. She would cook the pasta and warm the garlic bread after Chris arrived. Lori checked her emails while she waited. Another one from her boss asking for an update on when she would be back at work. Lori could have gone back right after she handed Wolfgang over to Christopher, but she had no desire to return. 'Not for a while yet.' she typed and hit send.

Did she dress for dinner? Lori stood facing her closet and slid hangers one way and then the other. Her work clothes were business attire, but they reminded her too much of her day job. She decided on a pair of black leggings, a long-sleeved T-shirt, and a silk scarf patterned in bright yellows, reds, oranges and turquoise. Lori folded the square fabric on the diagonal and tied it around her waist, with the knot over her right hip. It worked. Her reflection in the full-length mirror on her closet door appeared classy. Now for some accessories.

She selected bracelets with beads and gems that matched the colours in the scarf. The jewellery covered about three inches of her right forearm. The same style of wristlets surrounded her chunky watch on her left. Those, coupled with the long sleeves, kept her scars well hidden. Chris had seen them, so why was she so adamant about keeping them covered? Lori found a pair of plain gold hoops and put them in her ears just as the doorbell buzzed.

Thirty Seven

Lori's apartment, Calgary, Alberta

June 2, 2016

Lori answered the door expecting to see Chris and Wolfgang. Instead, Gary barged in.

"Wh-what are you doing here?"

"Now, Abi, you're not that naive, are you?" He slammed the door so hard that it banged shut and bounced back.

She turned to run, but he grabbed her by the arm and squeezed it.

"Let go! You're hurting me!"

"You ruined my life, you ungrateful little …."

"I had nothing to do with that. You did it yourself. Janey and I ensured you didn't wreck anyone else's lives as you did ours. I wish they would have locked you up, and thrown away the key. Better yet, stuck you in general population. No matter how heinous their crimes are, I hear the other prisoners hate pedophiles."

Lori willed Chris to get there. Gary twisted her arm behind her back and shoved her toward the bedroom.

"You're going to pay for me spending twenty years of my life behind bars." He pushed her backwards on the bed and jammed his knee between her thighs. His weight on the scarf she had put around her hips trapped her against the mattress.

Gary unbuckled his belt and yanked it free from the loops. He wrapped it around her wrists and the iron headboard, securing her hands above her head. Gary was going to rape her. Lori tried to scream, but he covered her mouth with his free hand. She squirmed and got his hand away, and she bit down on the tender skin between his thumb and index finger.

"You little ...," he growled.

She bit him hard enough that she drew blood.

He shook his hand, sending blood droplets through the air, and then slapped her hard across the face. She closed her eyes and whimpered. Those awful times when she was a little girl rushed back into her mind. He wasn't violent back then, but rough.

She struggled to break free but could not succeed. Did she lie back and relax? Let him have his way with her? It made her want to vomit.

The door was ajar when Chris arrived at Lori's apartment. Maybe Lori left it open, so he didn't have to knock when he arrived? He could come straight in. Chris warned her about that when she called him, freaking out because Gary was on the street outside her apartment.

Wolfgang's leash remained in the truck. Chris had removed it when he put the dog in the vehicle. He didn't bother putting it back on to walk the short distance from where he parked to Lori's apartment since the Great Dane was well-behaved.

Wolfie's hackles rose, and he growled. Something was wrong. Chris pushed the door open, and the dog raced into the apartment. Was Lori hurt? He checked the bathroom, living room, and kitchen. The contents of the unattended pot on the stove had burned. He switched off the element and slid the vessel to the back of the ceramic cooktop. The only room she could be in was the bedroom.

The dog's growls got louder. Chris put his ear to the door. A faint noise like muffled crying became audible. Then, he turned the knob and gave a push. Wolfgang charged through the slight opening, snapping and snarling.

Chris was right behind the Great Dane. He wrapped Lori's assailant in a choke hold, yanked him away from her, and shoved him into the chair in the corner. "Are you okay? Did he hurt you?" he asked Lori.

"N-not for lack of trying."

He turned to the dog. "Wolfgang guard," he commanded, then turned his attention to unbinding her wrists. Once Chris freed her, he said, "Call 9-1-1." He held out his cell phone.

Lori scrambled off the bed.

"There's an awful lot of blood in here. Are you sure you're okay?"

"The little bitch bit me," Gary said.

"First responders are on their way," she said as she returned the phone to Chris.

He pulled her into his arms, kissed her forehead, and held her.

"I can't stay here any longer. Gary found me. It isn't safe anymore. I have to leave," Lori said. Christopher steered her out of the bedroom to the living room and the couch. She sat cross-legged on the sofa and rocked back and forth as she spoke.

"Hey, call off your dog." Gary yelled from the bedroom. Wolfgang's growls grew louder.

"Not happening," Chris said.

Chris let the first responders into the apartment when the intercom buzzed.

She stopped rocking and looked towards the door.

Once the police arrived and secured the scene, two paramedics — one male and one female — followed and rushed straight to Lori's side.

She leapt off the sofa and paced the room, unable to stand

any close contact with anyone, and continued repeating those same four sentences. "I can't stay here any longer. Gary found me. It isn't safe anymore. I have to leave."

"Can you tell us what happened?" one officer asked.

Chris guided Lori to a chair and sat on the arm.

"M-my u-uncle. A-attacked m-me." Lori touched her fingertips to her face where he had slapped her. It hurt like crazy.

"Where is your uncle now?"

"B-bedroom."

"Aren't you afraid of him coming out and going after you again?" asked the other police officer.

"Not with Wolfgang guarding him," said Chris. He got up, but Lori grabbed his arm.

"And just who and what is Wolfgang?"

"My Great Dane."

The other officer opened the bedroom door. Lori's eyes followed his movements. With the room no longer closed off, Wolfie's growls were louder.

Chris stood. "You're okay," he said to her.

"But ...."

"It's okay. I'm just getting Wolfgang. You've got a police officer and two paramedics with you. I'll be right back."

Lori shrank into the chair trying to disappear.

A minute later, Chris and the dog returned. Soon after that, the cop who entered her bedroom guided Gary out, his hands cuffed behind his back.

"His name is Gary McNeil. He did twenty years for abusing his daughter, Janey, and me. Not just any abuse. Sexual abuse. He found me at Lake Louise near the Chateau a few weeks ago."

The cop leading Lori's uncle asked his partner to radio for backup and removal of the suspect from the apartment.

Once Gary was out of the way, the police officers spoke to Lori and got her statement recorded on his cell phone regarding the current assault. "When and where did the childhood abuse take place?"

"It started when I was ten, and he lived at our house. Aunt

Cindy had already kicked him out for abusing his daughter. She was younger than that. We're the same age. Our birthdays are a week apart. I lived in Yorkton, Saskatchewan, at the time, and she lived in Regina. In those days, my name was Abigail Laurie Brownell. I changed it to Lori Brownlee in 1993 after I started at Lakeland College."

"Thank you. That's most helpful." He turned the recording off.

Then they talked to Chris.

The paramedics treated her. "No cuts. Blood pressure up. Severe contusion to the face." The one medic probed her cheek, and she winced. "No broken bones from what I can tell, but an x-ray will confirm. The eye is bloodshot, but the retina seems to be intact." The bright flashlight in her face made Lori blink.

"Can you walk to the ambulance?" The female first responder asked.

"I don't want to be hospitalized."

The police were done with Chris. "Can I go with her?"

"Do you have a vehicle?"

"Yeah, why?"

"Why don't you follow behind? That way, you can bring her home once she's released."

"Okay." Chris hugged Lori and kissed her forehead. She clung to him. "It's okay. I'll be right behind you."

"What about Wolfie?" she asked.

"He'll be fine for a while. Wolfgang. Bed." The Great Dane disappeared into the bedroom.

"Can I stay with her at the hospital?"

"Are you her next of kin?"

"Yes," Christopher lied.

Lori let the paramedics take her to the ambulance. Outside, a crowd had gathered.

Chris ensured he had Lori's purse, which he hoped contained her health card and other identification. He grabbed the keys from the table and closed the apartment door. This evening took an unexpected and unwanted turn. If he and Wolfie had only arrived at her home sooner. He might have been able to prevent the attack.

His success rate at protecting damsels in distress or otherwise was non-existent — Marianne all those years ago, and now Lori.

The medics didn't consider her case an emergency since she was mobile and alert, so the lights and siren were off, and he could keep up. Once, they got separated at a set of traffic lights. The ambulance got through, and he didn't, but he caught up to them. At least the traffic was light.

It took about fifteen minutes to drive from Lori's to Rockview General. Chris pulled into a parking bay across from the emergency department and walked to the ambulance. They were unloading Lori when he arrived. They took her straight through because she came by medical transport. The female paramedic recited the examination and her vitals while she was en route to the hospital. She was only away from him when they took her for x-rays.

"I can't go back there. I'm sorry. It isn't safe. Don't make me go back, please."

The fear in her voice broke Chris's heart. He knew that fear all too well. He had suffered nightmares after Marianne's death. The shooter was going to kill him and his family. "Why don't we do this? Once you're released, we'll go back to the hotel. I'll get my stuff and check out and stay with you. Sleep on the couch. That way, I'm right there if you need me. Besides, at least one of us has to go because we left Wolfie at your place."

"You come to stay with me, but you sleep in the bedroom, and I'll sleep on the couch. I cannot go back inside that room."

"You drive a hard bargain, Lori Brownlee."

The emergency room staff released Lori about nine-thirty. One nurse gave her some meds, while in the E.R., but Christopher didn't know what they were. Pain and maybe something to calm her? She was still shaking when they arrived at the hospital. How they got a clear x-ray, he didn't know. But all was well on that front. No broken bones. No damage to her eye.

They'd given her pills to help her sleep later that evening, but the instructions were not to take them until she went to bed. For her pain, she only needed Tylenol. She could use an icepack on her cheek but make sure she wrapped it in a towel and did not leave it on her face too long.

Chris had absorbed all the instructions, and he pocketed the pills they sent home with her. He would administer them and keep them safe. He still didn't like the idea of putting Lori out of her bed. Still, he understood her reasoning behind not wanting to be in her room.

"Oh, my God! The spaghetti sauce. I never turned it off," Lori said as Chris helped her into the truck.

"Don't worry. I did when I got there and moved it off the burner."

"Supper is ruined. I wanted it to be special."

"You're safety is more important than a meal. Let's go get my stuff and take you home."

It didn't take long to gather his belongings from the hotel room. He had bought nothing except for toiletries he ran out of. He only had what was in the duffel bag he took when he left for his last trip to the work camp.

Thirty-Eight

Lori's apartment, Calgary, Alberta

June 2, 2016

Christopher opened the apartment door, Lori clinging to his arm. Wolfgang stood on the opposite side, tail wagging. "Let us get inside, Wolfie." He nudged the dog with his thigh so they could enter.

"You said you had news earlier?"

"It seems like a lifetime ago now, after everything that's happened. Let me get you settled on the couch, and I'll tell you." Chris pulled the blanket off the back of the sofa and wrapped the throw around Lori's shoulders. "You hungry? I might be able to salvage the sauce."

"Not now. You don't need to fuss over me."

His mother said those exact words when he stayed behind after the rest of his siblings returned to their homes after their father's funeral. He didn't see it as fussing then and didn't now. He cared a great deal about Lori.

She reached out and grabbed his hand. "Tell me your news, Christopher Scott."

He sat beside her. "I spoke with my insurance company earlier today for the umpteenth time. I'm covered for wildfires."

"That's wonderful!" Lori threw her arms around him and hugged him, pressing her bruised cheek against his face. She pulled back. "Ouch. Shouldn't have done that."

Chris planted the softest kiss possible on her injury, then pulled her close again, ensuring her uninjured cheek was next to his face.

"I have some news, too," Lori said as she tucked her legs on the couch under the blanket.

"Tell me." Chris held her hands in his, brought them to his mouth, and kissed them.

"I phoned my mother this morning. I called early enough that I got her before she left for work." She pulled her hands out of Christopher's and rubbed her thighs. "Not the reaction I hoped for but the one I expected."

"I'm sorry," Chris said, and kissed her uninjured cheek.

"My father had a heart attack and subsequent open heart surgery. I want to phone again and speak to him. He's due home on the fourth. I hope he won't be as cold as my mother was."

"I'm sorry you had to go through that." He tucked an errant lock of hair which had fallen in her face behind her ear.

"Grandpa Brownell died a couple of years ago, and my brother Ricky inherited the farm. My mom got in another dig when she said at least it remained in the family. Speaking of that, I left my address book on the kitchen table. I want to call the farm and talk to my brother. Can you bring it to me?"

"Sure."

After Chris left the room, Wolfgang laid his chin on Lori's lap. She buried her face on his head between his pointy ears and drew in a ragged breath. How had her life gone so wrong? Why her? She didn't deserve that fate, did she?

"Here you go," Chris said as he handed the spiral-bound book to her. "This was on the floor." He held out the discoloured photo.

"Where did you find that?" Lori snatched the picture away from him.

"On the floor under the table. Let me see it."

She handed the image to him. She never liked it. Never enjoyed having her picture taken. After Chris showed her the photograph of his almost fiancée, she hated this one even more. She must have knocked this off the table when she returned the other things to the box.

Lori punched the phone number for the farm into her cell phone. Almost immediately, a recording said the number was no longer in service. "So much for that idea. The number doesn't work anymore."

"I'm sorry. I know you wanted to talk to your brother. Why don't we drive to the farm and back tomorrow?"

"Too far. It takes almost a day just to get there, and then we'd have to come back afterwards. No, I'll think of something else."

"The farm wouldn't have moved, so you could always write to him."

"That's a wonderful idea. Why didn't I think of that?"

"But not tonight. You've had a rough day. You need sleep."

Chris gave Lori one of the pills she received from the hospital and tucked her in and made her comfortable. "I don't mind sleeping out here."

"And I don't want to sleep in *that* room."

"Your water is on the table if you need it." Chris walked through the apartment, turning off the lights. He positioned the chain on the latch when he locked the door. Wolfgang raised his head when he walked by the opening between the foyer and the living room, but dropped it down again.

Before he turned out the ceiling light in the kitchen, Chris scooped as much sauce as he could salvage into a container, and placed it in the fridge. He put the pot to soak in the sink filled with hot, soapy water, and finished with a quick tidying of the room.

Chris turned on the ceiling light and shut the bedroom door. He didn't wear pyjamas or anything to bed — preferred to sleep au naturel. However, he was sharing the apartment and Lori had been through a traumatic experience earlier in the evening, so Chris left on his boxers. No need to make her think he had ulterior motives. He opened the door a crack and turned out the light.

He pulled back the blankets, sat on the bed, and raked his fingers through his hair, then swung his legs up and under the sheets, and pulled the covers up to his chest. He folded his hands behind his head and stared at the ceiling.

Would Lori ever trust him one hundred percent? He doubted it because of everything she had been through. The prison or parole authorities attached conditions to her uncle's release from prison. How about staying away from the victims, for a start? By now, her uncle should be returned to jail where he would remain for a long time. Chris threw back the covers, grabbed his jeans from the chair in the corner, and laid them on the bed. If Lori needed him in the night, getting to her was paramount — appearing in his underwear was not the thing to do.

Lori tossed and turned on the sofa, unable to find a comfortable position. She gave up and sat with the covers around her shoulders. Wolfgang snored on the bed she had bought for him. Those nights he stayed with Chris at the hotel were lonely. She'd had him to herself for some time before reuniting the dog and its owner. What would have happened if Wolfie had been with her when her uncle barged in and attacked her? A bloodbath, judging by the dog's reaction when he charged into her bedroom.

She sipped her water. Chris told her it was too late to write to her brother, but since she couldn't sleep, she might as well. Had her mother called Ricky and told him about their phone conversation? Lori hadn't wanted to shut her family out, but it was the only way she ensured no one spilled the beans of her new identity to Uncle Gary.

Lori pulled out the lined paper from the end table drawer and turned on the lamp. Wolfgang lifted his head. She found a pen clipped to a crochet pattern book on the coffee table. She made herself comfortable and wrote.

Hi Ricky,

There's so much I need to tell you. I don't even know if you'll open this letter or just toss it in the trash without giving it a second glance when you see who wrote it. I'm hoping you'll read my note. No doubt Mom has contacted you by now and told you I got in touch. There was a reason for that silence.

You must remember when the police arrested Uncle Gary and charged him with the sexual abuse of Janey and me. I was terrified he'd find me after his release from prison, and the abuse would start all over again.

Just after I started at Lakeland, I changed my name. All nice and legal like. Along with that, I changed my appearance — grew my hair long, and started wearing contacts. You wouldn't recognize me now.

I suppose Mom also told you she saw me rescuing a dog from the Fort Mac wildfire on TV. Maybe you saw me, too. His owner is the kindest, gentlest man I know after dad, and you, of course.

Anyway, my fears of Uncle Gary finding me after his release weren't unfounded. I chose to return the dog to its owner at Lake Louise because of the crowds. Chris (the Great Dane's owner) and I were the only ones who knew. Uncle Gary was there, even before Chris arrived. He couldn't leave the oil sands until the officials evacuated his work camp on May 16th. I still cringe when I hear those two words Gary said to me. "Hello, Abi." And then there was the smell of that cologne he used.

Worst of all, he found out where I live and forced his way into my apartment tonight. I thought he was going to kill me. I've never seen him that angry. Ricky, he scared me more than he's ever done before. I don't know who to turn to or where to go if Chris isn't around. He would and has helped me, but what happens if he can't? What happens if he's away at the oil sands? I know you're far away from where I live, but I'd like to think you would help me if I needed it.

Are you married now? If so, would I like your wife? Do you have kids and how many? Grandpa Brownell's death saddened me. I'm glad he left the farm to you. You loved it so much. I was the indoor girl there. Grandma's molasses cookies and hugs were what I liked best about the place. Is the stuffed barn owl still in the front room? The pocket doors separating the living and dining rooms, the tin walls and ceiling in the kitchen, are they still there, too? Let's not forget the endless food when we went. We were just little kids when she died, but I still remember our parents saying she catered her own funeral. She was always making something and tucking it away in the freezer for church dinners, funerals or weddings; whatever the occasion, something made by Grandma Brownell was a staple.

You'd like Chris. He's a good man. If you have other family, please say hello to them from me. And phone or text me sometime. But only if you want to. My number is 403-555-1212.

Your sister,
~~Abigail~~ Lori

Lori read and reread the letter. Happy with everything she said, she addressed an envelope to Ricky but hesitated about the return address. In the end, she used her birth name along with her location. After the earlier incident, if her uncle wasn't in jail, he should be. It was a matter of days before she left the city with Chris.

She curled back up on the couch and hoped she hadn't disturbed him, and this time, sleep overtook her when her head hit the pillow.

Chris woke and looked around the room. Where was he? Then he remembered he was at Lori's apartment. What was that noise? Crying? He tossed the covers aside, snatched his jeans from the foot of the bed, and tugged them on. Lori was having a nightmare. He started for the door, but stopped. Rather than go out without a shirt, he grabbed his T-shirt from the chair and pulled it over his head.

Lori was curled up in a ball on the couch with her arms wrapped around her abdomen, her body wracked by convulsive sobs. Chris reached out and touched her shoulder. She lashed back with flailing arms. "Lori, you're okay. It's me, Chris," he whispered, trying to avoid getting struck. He moved back. How could he wake her without being injured or her injuring herself?

Wolfgang stirred on his bed at the opposite end of the couch. The Great Dane stood, stretched, and walked to the sofa near Lori. Chris feared the reaction between her and the animal, but the dog walked past her and sat beside him.

"Lori. You're dreaming. Wake up. It's Chris. I'm right here. So is Wolfie." He murmured, so he didn't frighten her. She hugged her stomach again. That was a good thing. At least if she kept her arms otherwise occupied, she wouldn't be hitting him.

Chris reached up and turned on the table lamp. Maybe if he illuminated the room, she would wake less frightened, and he could help her. It took a few moments, but her eyelids flickered, and she opened her eyes.

"Wh-what are you doing out here?" Lori asked.

"You were having a nightmare," Chris replied. He eased her into a sitting position, sat beside her, and wrapped his arm around her shoulders. "Want to tell me about it?"

She drew in a shuddering breath, shook her head, and kept her arms wrapped around her waist.

"Are you in pain?"

Lori nodded.

"Do you want something for it? Tylenol? Advil?" After he asked about the painkillers, he realized they were not a good idea, given the drugs they gave her at the hospital. "Is it because of what Gary did to you earlier when he broke into your apartment?"

"N-no."

That was something.

"H-he p-punched m-me."

"Gary?"

Again, Lori nodded.

"But you said …." The dream had to be related to an event in her past if it were because of Gary. How to persuade her to tell him?

"Why did he punch you?"

"I-I b-bit him."

That explained the bruise on her face, but not the sore stomach.

"Why did you bite him?"

"H-he st-stuck it in m-my m-mouth. I-I d-didn't l-like it. I-it m-made me ch-choke."

That pig! He deserved to get bitten. Chris didn't push any further. He had a decent idea of where she sunk her teeth in, and he cringed. He bundled Lori into his arms and comforted her.

Thirty-Nine

Lori's apartment, Calgary, Alberta

June 3, 2016

Lori woke first and padded out to the kitchen. After yesterday, she expected to find a mess to clean up. But, when she turned on the ceiling light, a sparkling clean room greeted her and the sauce pot in the sink.

After he got her settled in on the couch, Chris had cleaned up the kitchen. She appreciated the gesture. Her mind was foggy from the pill she took the previous night, and she didn't like the sensation. The fogginess made her feel out of control like when she was little. Had her uncle drugged her?

She puttered around the apartment, trying not to make much noise, so she didn't wake Chris. Her efforts were for naught. The toilet flushed, and moments later, he appeared in the doorway.

"How are you feeling this morning?" he asked.

"A bit foggy. Can't say, I like the sensation."

"How did you sleep?"

"Like the dead. Once I resolved what was on my mind."

"You don't remember the nightmare? It woke me. I stayed

up with you until you fell back asleep."

Nightmares were commonplace to Lori. Over the years, she experienced so many she lost track. She recalled being in Chris's arms but thought she had dreamt it. "No. I took you up on your suggestion and wrote a letter to my brother. I want to mail it today. I'm eager to find out if he'll respond, so I included my cell number and asked him to phone or text me. I'd like to think he will, but I wouldn't be surprised if Mom turned him against me."

Chris enveloped her in a hug. "I can't see that happening." He kissed the top of her head.

She wanted to stay in his powerful arms forever — safe — and never leave and wouldn't except her cell phone rang.

A few minutes later, she returned to the kitchen. "That was the police. The one who came here last night. They've returned Uncle Gary to prison. Breaking conditions of his release, plus the charges from this latest incident. I hope he never gets out, but I'm not holding my breath. I mean, he got out the last time."

"You worry too much, although I understand where you're coming from."

Chris didn't know if he wanted to return to Fort Mac and his job at SUNCOR. When he was with Lori, he could protect her. Back working his two weeks on, two weeks off rotation, there would be a fourteen-day stretch where she would be alone. If Frank came home, she could turn to him if needed, but would they come back? He'd bet a lot wouldn't return for fear of another wildfire or, worse, a disaster at the oil sands. Until the fire, the most excitement was when the shovel operator dug up a section of a dinosaur fossil in 2011.

That discovery wreaked havoc on their work. First, they cordoned off the section where the worker made the find. At the same time, SUNCOR employees and specialists from the Royal Tyrrell Museum worked to excavate the monstrous find with as little damage as possible.

It was an exciting discovery, and from then on, everyone

walked with their eyes to the ground looking for other signs of unusual formations in the earth. Shawn became an overnight celebrity thanks to his discovering the remains of the ankylosaur.

If only Chris worked a regular job where he was home every night. He had done that before the nutcase gunned Marianne down and hated it. No, this job suited him well. He hoped that if he and Lori made a life together, his career would serve her, too.

Chris moved around the kitchen as if he lived in the apartment. He started a pot of medium roast to brew and took mugs out of the cupboards.

"You didn't need to do that. I can make a pot of coffee."

A cell phone chirped.

Chris pulled his cell phone out of his pocket. No calls, texts or messenger notifications. "Must be yours," he said.

Lori found her phone on the end table where she left it when she went to bed the night before. A red bubble with the number one overlapped the text message icon. No way it could be from Ricky; she hadn't mailed her letter yet, unless her mother gave him the number. It might have come up in the call display on their phone. If they had moved out of the dark ages from the black wall phone in the back hall outside the kitchen.

The message was from Janey.

The police called us last night asking if Dad came here. Said he attacked you.

He did, but he's back in jail. He breached conditions of his release and for his attack on me.

I know what he did to us years ago was wrong, but that? I thought they rehabilitated him while he was in the pen.

Lori wasn't the most adept at selfies, but she took one, showing the handprint-shaped bruise on her face and attached the picture to her return message.

Well? Think he was incapable of this?

Three bouncing dots on her phone's screen showed Janey was typing her reply. Chris brought her a cup of fresh brewed medium roast and placed it in front of her.

"It's Janey. The police were wondering if Gary had turned up in Regina. I'm guessing she means before he turned up here in Calgary."

Holy sh*t! I'm so sorry. I didn't think he would do that.

Lori threw her head back. Was her cousin that naïve? Her first thought was stupid, but she chose the more charitable description. Her uncle, Janey's father, had messed them both up. She had not seen Janey since the early 1990s, and then she looked like skin stretched over a skeleton. Her anorexia and bulimia had taken their toll on her body. That was besides the mental toll of Gary's actions on her.

Janey had spent time in the hospital because of her eating disorder. After that, the doctors transferred her to an in-patient facility that dealt with her cousin's issues. During her stays in rehab, they didn't allow contact with the outside world. The logic behind their decision was to prevent exposure to what put you in the clinic in the first place, so it was better to not go home or see visitors.

While Lori drank her coffee, Chris made breakfast. He was too good to her. She was a mess after suffering years of abuse from a man who held a position of authority over her. What would have happened if Chris and Wolfgang didn't arrive when they did? Gary would have raped her, and maybe even killed her. His hatred-filled eyes glared at her when he burst into her apartment.

Chris placed a plate of bacon and eggs in front of her and topped up her coffee before sitting down with his meal.

"We have to mail my letter to my brother," she said as she placed her mug on the table. "I need to buy stamps, so I'll get them at the drug store."

"Where do you want to go?"

"There is a Shoppers Drug Mart about a twenty-minute walk from here on 17 Avenue. There are others, but I know this one sells stamps, and they have a mailbox outside the entrance."

"Do you want to walk, or rather I drive you?" Chris asked.

"Walk. The fresh air will clear my head, I hope."

Then it hit her. Her face. That handprint-shaped bruise needed to be covered. Would people think Chris did that to her? She could wear her oversized Oakley sunglasses. They'd hide a good portion of the souvenir her uncle left her with.

Sometimes, life sucked, and other times, it was fantastic. However, since meeting Chris, the latter took the top spot.

"You go get dressed and do whatever you need to do, and I'll clean up here."

"You don't have to do that. I'll look after it. You made breakfast," Lori protested.

He ignored her objections. Chris cleared the table and had water running in the sink to wash the dishes. She'd love to meet his mother since the woman did an excellent job raising her son and making him a kind and compassionate man.

Lori left the room, gathered some clean clothes, and headed for the shower. At least here, unlike back in Yorkton, you could run water in two places and not lose water pressure or scald yourself.

Standing before the bathroom mirror, she hunted through her makeup bag. She had concealer, but where was it? The two tubes had fallen to the bottom since she never used them often. Now which one to use for which. Was it yellow to hide the red capillaries? Or was it green? No. Yellow for the dark under-eye bags and green for the others.

It took a long time, but Lori got her makeup done and hid the handprint in its lovely shades of black and blue. The tenderness of her cheek compounded the problem because it hurt so much when she applied any pressure, no matter how light.

"Ready?" she called to Christopher in the kitchen. Lori pulled on her zip-front hoodie and left the hood up, and put on her sunglasses. Her reflection in the mirror over the small table in the foyer said she did an excellent job on the makeup.

Chris joined her, put Wolfgang's leash on him, and the three set out for the pharmacy.

Forty

Calgary to Beacon Hill, Fort McMurray, Alberta

June 4, 2016

The day of reckoning had arrived and the Beacon Hill residents could return home. Whether they had a house to return to was a different story. Christopher had been in contact with Frank when he and Wolfgang were reunited. The news was a massive relief to the Connolly family.

He had asked Lori to go home with him to Fort Mac. It was a spur-of-the-moment comment, but he was glad he did it. She would be company for him on the long drive north. They planned to leave her apartment at about seven, which would put them at his house around three that afternoon, depending on traffic which could be bottlenecked getting into Fort McMurray.

"I want to call my father before we leave. Is that okay?"

Chris couldn't very well refuse. He would be a terrible person if he did.

"Go ahead. Just don't be too long."

Lori slipped into the bedroom and closed the door halfway. It was not so much that she didn't want Chris to overhear her conversation with her father. She just wanted it to be the two of them — a proper father-daughter chat.

She punched in the number and waited for the connection to go through. It was early in the morning, so she hoped the man was home, and she wouldn't be disturbing him. He may have gone to bed when he finished his run. After a number of days driving his transport, he might be sitting at the kitchen table having a coffee.

After about the tenth ring, someone answered.

"Hello."

Her father. "Hi, Dad. It's me, Abigail, but I go by Lori now."

"Abigail, my dear girl. How are you?"

"I should ask that about you. Mom told me you had a heart attack and open heart surgery. Are you okay?"

"I'm all the better now, hearing your voice."

"Did she tell you I called her the other day?"

"Yes. I realize things were fraught between you and your mother over Gary's actions and her disbelief a relative of hers could do such a terrible thing. I hope one day you'll be able to make up."

"Maybe." It would take a lot to convince Lori she and her mother would ever patch things up. "Mom said you saw me on TV."

"Yes, we did. Whatever possessed you to put your life in danger like that?"

"I couldn't leave that dog there to die."

"Yes, you always dragged home injured birds and whatnot when you were a little girl. I supposed I expected nothing else from you."

"Dad, I've met a wonderful man. He's the owner of the dog. He's kind and caring and gentle, like someone else I know. You."

Her father's voice cracked.

"I'm sorry to hear about Grandpa Brownell."

Chris stood at the door opening and pointed to his watch.

"I have to go, Dad. Chris is eager to get on the road. I'm going back to Fort McMurray with him," she babbled. "Oh, and if you're talking to Ricky, tell him I tried to call. The number I have for the farm isn't any good anymore, so I wrote him a letter. Mailed it yesterday. Bye, Dad. Love you. Gotta go."

Lori disconnected her call. Her father didn't judge her, nor had he made her feel guilty, unlike her mother.

"I'm ready," she said as she exited the bedroom.

Chris stood to one side so she could leave the apartment with Wolfgang, then pulled the door shut and handed Lori her keys.

He opened the doors on the passenger side of the truck. She stowed her bag and then climbed into the seat. Wolfgang jumped into the back and stuck his head between the seats, and she petted him. "Hey, Wolfie."

The Great Dane inched forward. "No, Wolfgang. Back in the backseat. There's no room up here." Christopher slid behind the wheel.

Despite it being early Saturday morning, the traffic was heavy. It seemed worse than other days. That could have been because of the long drive he had to make and he wanted to get moving. Eight hours in perfect conditions. Over ten in the real world.

"Penny for them," Lori said after about twenty minutes of silence.

"Just thinking about what I'm returning to." Chris sighed.

"You've heard nothing from anyone?"

"Everyone was in the same position except for the skeleton crew. We're all returning to the unknown."

Lori placed her hand on his thigh. "It will be okay. I know it will."

Be okay. Like that was ever going to happen. It didn't occur when Marianne died. He swore she'd be okay, and look where that got her. Dead. Nothing would ever be all right again. Lori believed in him. What a joke.

He liked Lori. He wanted her — baggage, warts and all. Her past messed her up like his did to him. They had different causes but messed up all the same, so it made them perfect for one another.

Wolfgang whined. "Can you hang on until we get a rest area? I'd rather not have to pull off onto the shoulder for you. We can all stretch our legs at the rest areas."

After four-thirty, they reached Fort McMurray. Atop one overpass, two fire trucks flew a Canadian flag between them from their extended ladders. Off-duty firefighters stood and waved to everyone who approached. A lump formed in Lori's throat. The men and women who had worked for weeks with little rest welcomed the people back home.

She stole a glance at Christopher. His eyes were glassy with tears. He had spoken little the entire time they travelled from Calgary to here. The closer they got, the more silent he became. Her heart ached for him. Whatever the outcome, she was there for him.

Chris made the turn onto his street in Beacon Hill. Houses on one side of the road survived unscathed but their vinyl siding had melted into bizarre shapes. Fridges and freezers stood at the curb outside homes whose owners had already arrived. Straps held them closed, to prevent the stench of the decaying food inside from escaping, thus keeping wild animals away. The opposite side of the street — destroyed. Not a single house stood — all burned to their foundations. Burnt-out vehicles sat in some driveways belonging to families who owned two or more vehicles, but when they evacuated, only took one. The area looked like a war zone, except it wasn't bombs that destroyed the houses. It was the fire, which was probably preventable.

About halfway down the street, Chris pulled over. He eased out of the truck, massaged the back of his neck, and leaned against the truck's box. Frank's house stood. That would be a relief for them. They weren't back yet. No vehicle in the driveway and no appliances on the side of the street. He never asked where they were, when he contacted his neighbour advising of Wolfgang's safety. He enquired after them, their health, how the girls were coping, but not where they went. Chris pulled out his phone and typed.

You'll be glad to know your house is still in one piece, so when are you coming home?

He returned his phone to the case on his belt.

Lori joined him, and he draped his arm around her shoulder.

"Which one is yours?"

He dropped to the ground and sat with his back against the truck. She sat next to him and laid her head on his chest. "I'm sorry."

Christopher knew this would be the outcome, although he didn't count on Frank's house and others on that side of the street still standing. His cell phone pinged, and he took it out of the holster.

Thanks for the update. Not sure when we'll be home. We're at the in-laws in Winnipeg. What about your house?

Gone. Burnt to the ground. Christopher texted back.

Sorry, man. Olivia doesn't think she'll come back soon, but the news about our place made her happy. Not sure I do either.

Christopher understood their apprehension. He harboured the same fears. Chris hadn't known Lori long, but she would never have to reinvent herself if he had any say in the matter. He would do his best to keep her safe. No matter where he called home, everything would work out as long as she was with him.

Epilogue

Near the Chateau Lake Louise, Alberta

May 18, 2017

On the first anniversary of their meeting, Chris planned a surprise. This past year had been eventful, and mostly in a good way. However, there were a few moments he'd just as soon forget — losing his house in the wildfire topped that list, followed by Gary's reappearance and assault on Lori.

He grinned. Lori would be thrilled — at least, he hoped so. Chris stole a glance towards the passenger seat. She was beautiful, and spending this last year with her was the best thing he had done.

He chose a route that would take them to their destination without giving Lori any advance knowledge. Further insurance to aid in the surprise happened when they were about five miles away; he blindfolded her. In order for his plan to work, she needed to be kept in the dark until they arrived.

Chris pulled the truck into the parking lot at Lake Louise. "Here we are. You can take off your blindfold now." He held his breath as he waited for her reaction.

Lori yanked the covering from her eyes. "Wh-where? Are

we where I think we are? Lake Louise?"

"Yes."

Chris stepped out of the truck, helped Lori down, and let Wolfgang out of the back seat. He took her hand, and they walked to the shore of the lake. He glanced around. Another part of the surprise should arrive soon.

"Why did you bring me here? I mean, after last year ...." Her raised voice said she was not happy about his choice of destinations.

"I plan on changing that for you. It was the day we first met. I'm hoping that's more important than the unpleasantness of your uncle turning up and acting like a jerk."

He took advantage of the situation when she turned her back. "Turn around," he said.

Lori turned. Chris was down on one knee, his arm extended, and a small velveteen box in his hand. He opened it, then took her hand in his.

"Will you do me the honour of becoming my wife? Mrs. Christopher Scott?"

She clapped her hands over her mouth. Chris's gesture left her speechless. She had enjoyed all her time with him since their first meeting a year ago. Lori had spent every hour possible in his company since they returned to Fort Mac and discovered Chris's house burnt to the ground. She helped him rebuild and worked for the bank, helping people get their lives back on track. Many of them didn't have the proper insurance coverage, so they had to start from scratch with lines of credit, loans and mortgages. Sometimes, they didn't receive a sufficient payout to rebuild and required extra money.

"Well?"

Lori snapped out of her reverie. "Yes! Yes! Me and my warts and everything will marry you."

Chris removed the ring from the box, slipped it on her finger, kissed her hand, and stood and hugged her.

Wolfgang nuzzled against Lori's thigh. She extended her arm and wiggled her fingers, making the diamond solitaire sparkle in the sunlight. It was perfect. Chris was perfect. On this day, Lake Louise was perfect. If only she could freeze this moment.

With his arm around her shoulders, they began walking away from the lakeshore. Part two of his surprise should be here unless they've reconsidered. He hoped not. They could run late — it was not unheard of. He was late when he met Lori a year ago, thanks to his taking the wrong exit and a multi-vehicle accident.

A couple approached from beyond the ridge. Was this them? His deception wouldn't please Lori, but if things went well, she'd forgive him. At least, he hoped she would. They drew closer. The man looked like a masculine version of Lori, so it must be Ricky.

"Oh my God, Ricky, is that you?" Lori asked. She ran, hindered by the old ankle injury.

The man quickened his pace. "Abs!" They embraced when they reached one another.

"How did you know I was here?"

"A little birdie told me," he shot a conspiratorial glance at Chris.

Lori turned to Christopher. "How did he know we would be here today? I didn't have a clue I would be here until we arrived."

Chris grinned.

"Chris?"

"Okay, I confess. I got your brother's number out of your phone and called him. I told him about today and asked him to meet us here."

Lori slapped Chris's arm and then hugged her brother again. She stood back, held her brother by his upper arms and said, "Aren't you going to introduce us?" She nodded to Ricky's female companion.

"This is my wife, Kimberly."

"Call me Kim." She stepped forward and shook Lori's hand, then enveloped her in a hug.

"My sister, who now goes by Lori. That will take some getting used to."

Chris stepped forward and shook both Kim's and Ricky's hands. "Chris Scott," he said.

"Who's looking after the farm? What about the cows?"

"This time of year, not much anymore. Grandpa sold his milk quota and the dairy herd. That's what tied us down in the past. It's now beef cattle, bison and cash crops like soybeans and canola. We were lucky and planted the fields about three weeks ago. But, we've also had some years where the ground is so wet we can't get on to work the land until late June."

With the way her brother spoke, the farm had transformed, and the changes made her sad. She wasn't as fond of it as Ricky, but it would never be the same as it was when she last visited.

"You guys will have to come to visit sometime."

Lori looked at Chris and said, "We'd love to."

"I've got some news about Uncle Gary," Ricky said.

"Never mention that man's name around me again."

"You will like this, I think. They didn't put him in protective custody when our dear, perverted uncle went back to the pen after he attacked you. General population this time. As they say, his reputation preceded him, and the other prisoners displayed their revulsion. And Uncle Gary is no more. He's dead. You'll never have to worry about him again." Ricky pulled his sister into a hug.

Lori smiled. Her life had gone full circle; she was going to marry a wonderful man, and her tormenter was dead. She might be able to put the past behind her and focus on her future.

Also by Melanie Robertson-King

The Consequences Collection
Tim's Magic Christmas
The Secret of Hillcrest House
A Shadow in the Past (second edition)
Shadows From Her Past
YESTERDAY TODAY ALWAYS
Cole's Notes (Revised version)
It Happened on Dufferin Terrace
It Happened in Gastown
It Happened at Percé Rock
All Aboard the Canadian with Buddy and his Four Fantastic
Furry Friends!
(King Park Press)

Cole's Notes (A Short Story)
EFD1: Starship Goodwords – a cross genre anthology
(CARRICK PUBLISHING, 2012)

Future Titles in the *It Happened* Series ...
featuring the Layne and Scott families

It Happened in Niagara Falls

MELANIE ROBERTSON-KING

https://melanierobertson-king.com

Melanie Robertson-King has always been a fan of the written word. Growing up as an only child, her face was almost always buried in a book from the time she could read. Her father was one of the thousands of Home Children sent to Canada through the auspices of The Orphan Homes of Scotland, and she has been fortunate to be able to visit her father's homeland many times and even met the Princess Royal (Princess Anne) at the orphanage where he was raised.

www.ingramcontent.com/pod-product-compliance
Lightning Source LLC
Chambersburg PA
CBHW070503260626
47161CB00004B/1432

* 9 7 8 1 9 9 0 3 7 1 0 6 6 *